A Pig's Ear

By Tony McLean

Crane Hill Publishing

Tony McLean

Text copyright © 2018 Tony McLean

All rights reserved

ISBN-9781795764414

1

Paisley was a town on its knees begging for mercy, the to-let signs above the closed department stores and plethora of pound shops testament to its failing status. The mercantile vultures were circling the skyline just waiting to tear at the tired flesh and peck the marrow from the brittle bones of the corpse. The most telling part of it all was the fact that when the pubs closed they stayed closed, no chain nor franchise altruistic or stupid enough to try and pump new life into the economic black hole that was running a bar in the once affluent mill town. Bertie Sweeney was neither altruistic nor stupid yet he managed and owned Bert's bar in the town's New Street. Unlike many of his countrymen he hadn't drank away the profits of his ailing pub, they had simply drained over the past five years. Countless times he'd considered taking what he could get for it (if anything) and returning to Kerry and the quiet life. That's why he enjoyed his Sunday morning walks in the Glennifer Braes, just him and his chocolate Labrador Revel. This early in the morning there was never another living soul around.

He threw the well bitten yellow tennis ball into the air and watched as the dog bolted after it. He wiped the greasy rain from his forehead before rubbing his hand through his hair to try and dry it. From here he could see out over the whole of the Glasgow conurbation, his vantage point allowing him the knowledge that it was teeming with rain from Dumbarton in the west to Steppes in the east. He heard the familiar roar of the cargo plane that exited Glasgow Airport at this time every day and watched as it made its uneven way into the clouds. He turned and headed for the bridge across the burn and along the dirt path that lead to the Car Park in the Sky. Halfway round a copse of fir trees he looked for the dog. Nowhere to be seen, probably chasing rabbits. 'Revel!' he barked. Before long the dog was back by his side, panting for him to throw the ball again. 'Here then ya daft bugger, give us it.' He took the ball from Revel's salivating jaw and threw it high into the air ahead. 'Go get it boy, go get it.'

He followed after the dog, the rain stinging his face and the moisture from the long grass soaking his denims. It was time to head home and tuck into some breakfast. His days of Sunday morning fry ups were long behind him - muesli, fruit and wholemeal toast awaited him. The thought of it didn't exactly put an extra spring in his step, but the rain did, he'd heard the forecast – it was to be heavy all day, with gale force winds to boot. It was August in the west of Scotland. He had a busy day ahead, normally Sundays were steady, quiet if he was being honest, but today St Mirren were playing Celtic and it was only on satellite. The start of the new football season and the bar would be rammed with dripping wet football fans, too skint to get either tickets or a dish attached to their homes. The thought of it cheered him as much as his health-conscious breakfast. He tramped out of the long grass and pointlessly shook himself off as his feet hit the well-worn dirt path. He snorted and expelled some phlegm back into the grass that had soaked his jeans. Now where was that bloody mutt? 'Revel!' He carried on walking towards the car park, the dog knew the way and would no doubt catch him up.

As he headed towards the play park there was still no sign of the dog. He looked behind and shouted. 'Revel!' He was surprised to find that the noisy barking came from behind him, from the car park. 'Jesus! How did you get there?' He started towards the dog, but it turned and ran the short distance to the only car in the place – a black Audi. There were never usually cars here this early, could be one of the hunting crowd trying to get that elusive early bird, Bertie thought, rather pleased with himself. He noticed that the dog was jumping up on the driver's side door. 'Revel! Leave the car alone for ...' He started walking quickly toward the car to control the dog, the hunting crowd normally took kindly to canines, but you never knew, someone with a car like that wouldn't take too well to anything scratching their paintwork. 'Revel! Come away ya daft...' He was about forty metres from the car and could see that there was no one inside. What was wrong with that bloody dog? He slowed down and looked at the car, not normally the chosen vehicle of choice of a hunter, the ferrets and lurchers would rip the interior to shreds. Bertie surmised it had been stolen and abandoned some time last night. At least the wee buggers had the good grace not to burn out a car of such capabilities, that, at least, showed a bit of respect. Maybe the world was becoming a better place, he thought to himself with a smile. He approached the car and went to grab the dog's collar. Something stopped him doing so. 'Jesus Christ! What the f...' He staggered back, almost tripping to the ground. The dog was still jumping up and barking at the driver's window. Bertie walked forward and grabbed the dog out the way before looking inside the car once more. He gasped, his eyes hadn't deceived him.

Bertie padded the pockets of his jacket and jeans even though he knew he hadn't brought his mobile with him, he never did when he was walking in the braes. He was regretting his decision now. 'Revel! Stupid bloody dog!' He grabbed the collar and pulled the dog to the ground to stop it pawing at the window. At a time like this Lassie would've been handy, but here he was stuck with this stupid mutt. 'Come on!' he rasped, starting to run whilst hunched over, holding the dog's collar. 'Got to get a phone!' The two of them ran out of the car park and made their way towards the Lugton Road. As he reached the road Bertie suddenly stopped running, the realisation that there was no hurry, she was definitely dead. He slowed his steps and started taking deep breaths to try and calm his racing heart – it was all over the place. There was no sound of any approaching cars, so he decided his best course of action was to walk down the road towards the twenty-four-hour garage. The rain had made the road greasy and he had a job keeping his feet as he descended the hill. When he was parallel with the top of the reservoir and the high-rise block he heard a screaming engine approaching, they always ripped it up on this road. He grabbed the dog and placed it on the verge to the side of him and began waving his hands in the air to attract the driver's attention. He was amazed that when the car rounded the blind bend it slowed considerably. First time, thought Bertie, this is a piece of pi… The car passed by him at just under thirty, the driver giving him the fingers and laughing. Bertie watched as twenty yards further down the hill the car picked up speed again. He realised now that it was only slowing for the speed camera. Tourist, thought Bertie. All the locals knew the speed cameras in the area had been painted over with black gloss by the boy racers.

A soaked through man and his best friend made their way across the garage forecourt. Bertie pulled at the door. It never opened, simply rattled. He walked over to the Perspex hatch and peered inside. No one about, so he rattled the dog's lead on the metal tray. 'Shop!'

He was about to shout again when he heard the sound of flushing from deep within the bowels of the shop. 'Okay, okay,' a muffled voice shouted.

'I hope you washed your hands,' Bertie said to the recalcitrant twenty-something lump that approached him, tucking in his creased red shirt into his black flannels as he did so. His monobrow eyes squinted to look through the plastic at Bertie, but his mouth just hung, saying nothing.

'You got a phone son?' Bertie snapped his fingers at the boy, hoping to prompt him back to reality. 'Phone the police. There's a woman been murdered up in the car park in the sky.'

2

The Phoenix housing complex to the west of the town had risen from the razed ashes of the former car plant that had provided gainful and worthy employment until the mid-seventies to the men (and occasional women) of Paisley and Linwood. Now the only employers on the site were mercantile, a supermarket the size of a few football pitches, clothing outlets of a similar size and somewhat ironically, more car showrooms than you could count on the fingers of one hand. The housing complex – all new build – bordered the notorious Ferguslie Park district of the town, but barring the occasional burglary when they had first been erected, the two areas kept their distance from each other. Not long after the first of the break-in's security guards could be seen wandering the quiet cul-de-sacs of The Phoenix checking for alien invaders. D.I. Rob Steele had been the last of the original tenants to set up home on the complex. Fifteen years ago, as an over-worked uniform policeman trawling the machete-strewn streets of a town under curfew from eleven at night, he had no time to think about a removal van and a couple of days off work. He bought the show home.

He padded from the shower to the bedroom and slumped face down on the bed. The nights on the drink were taking their toll. That was the trouble when things were slack at work, he found himself in the pub earlier and earlier each day. For him there was no joy to be found in chasing unnecessary targets just to keep some accountant happy. If there were no bad guys to catch, then there was no point in being at work. Do the job and finish, that was how it used to be, and in Steele's mind it was how it always should be. Mill Street was full of officers, many of whom had no idea what real police work involved, whose days were filled with charts, statistics and writing up reports on crime scenes they hadn't even been present at. He knew he was in danger of becoming a cliché, the office dinosaur, but the thought of people he could care less about sniggering behind his back certainly didn't keep him awake at night.

He sighed as he caught sight of himself in the wardrobe mirror. He had been six foot three of lumpen policeman in his prime and now look at him? He slapped his burgeoning gut a couple of times before drying his grey hair. It badly needed cut, and he promised himself he would get it done before he began to resemble Peter Stringfellow. It would do for another week or two. He heard the familiar sound of David Mansell's car pull up outside, a diesel people carrier, and dressed hurriedly. He opened the blinds and waved down at his colleague who signalled back then bent forwards towards the radio.

As Steele grabbed the passenger door he was distracted by some geese flying overhead, their low-flying V-formation having amazed him since his boyhood days. 'Oh to be that free, eh Dave?' His eyes nodded towards the birds.

'You're not kidding, out for a fly or examine some bloody murder? I know which I'd pick.' Mansell turned the radio down slightly; some band were trying too hard to be affected. 'Who's that?' Steele asked, the scorn in his voice almost palpable.

'I thought you'd like them boss,' Mansell concealed a smile behind his words. 'Got their latest CD in the glove compartment, can borrow it if you like.'

Steele's lips twitched, ready to bite his young colleague's head off until he realised his leg was being pulled.

'I know,' laughed Mansell. 'I know boss. If it's not The King or The Boss it would be a waste of time.'

'That's right, that's the way it was and shall be forever.'

'What about Prince?' asked Mansell, the glint in his eyes widening.

Steele said nothing, simply lifted an index finger in chastisement.

'Queen?' Mansell went through the gears after taking a left into Old Mill Road, heading towards the hospital.

Steele laughed, 'Nice try Dave. I'm not biting this morning.'

'Nearly had you though,' Mansell turned the car into Green Road and it came to a halt at the traffic lights at the junction of Corsebar and Lounsdale. 'No point putting on the ice cream sirens, eh?'

'Nah. She's dead son,' Steele said, before adding philosophically. 'She's dead now and she'll be dead when we get there.'

'You still pissed?' Mansell asked, realising his boss was jabbering like a drunk coming off a weekend bender. 'There's some mints in the glove compartment as well. No whisky though.' The lights changed and the car headed down Corsebar Road, the Royal Alexandria Hospital up the hill on the left-hand side, the cricket pitch on the right, where half a dozen gulls were taking their fill of the early morning worms at the wicket.

Steele popped two mints into his mouth and offered one to Mansell who refused. He placed them in his jacket pocket. Mansell coughed loudly. 'I'll buy you another packet. So what else do we know about this female?'

'That's it so far, that's all I've been told, got the call the same as you.' Mansell shifted the car into third as it started up the hill and stuck his foot to the floor. The gradient didn't allow him to get much over thirty however. Mansell hit the button and his window slid down, letting in the drizzle, the soaking preferable to the smell of Steele's breath, now sweet and sour *and* minty. 'Seems it was a guy out walking his dog who found her.'

'It's always a guy out walking his dog,' Steele laughed. 'Morning walkies should come with danger money.'

Mansell halted the car at the notorious junction of Moredun and Stanley Road, indicating right. Even this early in the morning he made absolutely certain it was safe to pull out and turned into Gleniffer Road. 'He never had a mobile though and had to go to the garage,' he pointed to the twenty-four-hour garage ahead. 'Apparently the guy was frantic on the phone, accused the dog walker of being the killer, screaming down the phone that he was getting away and generally being a tit. I mean, if he was our perp he wouldn't go squealing to the first person he comes across, would he?'

'Wouldn't think so, unless it was some elaborate double bluff played out by a criminal mastermind.' Steele smiled.

'In Paisley?' Mansell scoffed.

'And has somebody picked up this guy walking the dog?' asked Steele.

'Not heard boss.' Mansell replied. 'The Car Park in the Sky was a well-known dogging sight a few years ago. Nothing like that in your day, eh?'

'What do you mean? It's still "my day". Ask just about anybody at Mill Street and they'll tell you I'm the biggest five knuckle shuffler they know.' Steele pointed ahead to the garage. 'Pull in there.' he instructed Mansell.

With the Stanely reservoir to his right-hand side he indicated left and pulled up on the garage forecourt. The two men looked as a pallid faced male peered at them through the glass of the shop front. 'That'll be our terrified caller,' Steele sighed. 'He's got the look of someone ruined by masturbation. Let's get on with it.' He pushed the door open and stepped out of the car. He noted that the boy twitched as he made eye contact and looked away as though busy with something incredibly important. He tried the door, but as he thought, it was locked. He rapped the glass with his knuckles and held up his warrant card for the boy to look at.

'Have you caught him?' the boy asked as he nervously opened the door.

Steele frowned. 'Caught who?' He was somewhere between twenty-two and twenty-five, should be in his peak, in his prime, at his most gallus, thought Steele, yet here he was cowering like a pensioner.

'The killer!' The boy seemed to be almost at boiling point.

'I'm good son,' laughed Steele. 'Not that good though. Calm yourself and tell us about this guy that reported the crime.'

'He had hair and was tall and had a dog, a Labrador!' He boy squeaked nervously.

'Ahh!' Mansell sounded like he was auditioning for a coffee commercial. 'The tall, hairy Labrador killer. I think we've got enough sir,' he said to Steele, 'shall we go?'

Steele smiled, then a sudden memory entered his head. One from last night. He had been talking to a woman. A woman? How had that gone? Badly, obviously, he had woken alone. He jerked back to reality and shot his colleague a look. 'What I would like to know,' he sighed. 'Is where he went. What direction did he head in?'

The boy pointed. 'Back up the hill.'

'And when was this?'

'About half an hour ago.'

'Right.' Steele grabbed the boy's shoulders to reassure him. Another memory, he had held the woman's shoulders in the same manner. What had happened? 'Would that not tell you that he was not "the killer"? Maybe if you think back to earlier, go back as far as you like, midnight even, seen anything or anyone else that struck you as a wee bit suspicious?'

As the boy thought Steele released his grip from his shoulders and looked at the expression on his face. He was sure he could hear the cogs whirring in the numbnut's head.

'Maybe somebody covered in blood, acting furtively?' he suggested. 'Anything spring to mind?'

'Not really.' The boy shook his head. 'Quite a boring night, just the regulars wanting their Rizlas and munchies and taxi drivers and the like.'

'Taxi drivers and the like, eh?' Had there been a taxi together? Steele's mind was a blank. He thought long ago that he should start getting receipts for everything he did to enable him to retrace his drunken steps. 'Well, if anything does spring to mind, give me a call.' Steele handed over his card. 'And give us a couple of those pasties. I'm starving all of a sudden.' Had there been food? A soggy pizza? A racy kebab? He doubted it, there was no taste in his mouth other than rum. A small amount of fizzy cola, but mostly rum.

The boy headed to the pastries and came back and handed them over. Steele took them and turned on his heels leaving the boy with his hand out waiting for payment. 'We don't pay for things son,' Steele said without looking over his shoulder. 'We're the police.'

The boy's mouth gaped open, but as Steele opened the passenger side door his conscience got the better of him and he walked over to the metal tray and dropped a couple of pound coins in.

As he turned to walk away he heard the boy shout after him. 'You're a pound fifty short!'

Steele turned and threw another two pound coins into the tray. 'You should be wearing a mask! These better be bloody good.'

As the car exited the forecourt Steele opened one of the pasties and handed it to Mansell. He refused. 'No thanks boss,' he grimaced. 'You knock yourself out and have the two of them.'

'Fair enough,' Steele took a hefty bite out of his breakfast. 'Marvellous.' A spray of saliva and puff pastry soon decorated Mansell's windscreen.

Mansell caught sight of it. 'Oh aye, marvellous.'

They drove the rest of the distance to The Car Park in the Sky in silence.

When they got there Steele had polished off the first of his pasties and stuffed the wrapper into one of the empty plastic gaps on the inside door panel. Mansell stared at the offending wrapper as Steele got out, but his superior didn't notice. 'See the circus is already here,' he said, his arms resting on the roof of the car as he surveyed the scene. He instantly regretted it and took his arms off. The sleeves of his jacket were now wringing wet. He shook his head at the overuse of the blue and white crime scene tape. 'This is getting ridiculous,' he looked back into the car to see if Mansell was getting out. He was still staring at the discarded wrapper. Steele was oblivious. 'A spilt cup of tea in the canteen would merit two miles of tape and half a day's paperwork the way things are going son. God help us if it was soup! Mill Street would be closed for a week!' He looked back inside the car just as Mansell was getting out.

He looked across the top of the car at Steele. 'So?'

'A needle pulling thread. Boom, boom.' Steele held up his hand in apology, still drunk. 'Let's just see what unravels. That's all we'll be doing for the next few days, untangling her life then putting it all together again to see how it ended up in this.' He pointed towards the black Audi. A photographer had the passenger door open and was taking snapshots from every angle. There were half a dozen uniforms on site, but just one other detective, one of "The Two Johns", John McGlaughlin. Steele was surprised to see him here without his sparring partner, John Patterson. The two of them seemed joined at the hip. Steele called each of them "John Number Two" when he met them individually. He didn't know for sure if it rankled, but hoped it did. He waited for Mansell before walking towards the perimeter of the tape.

'Wonder what's wrong with The Other John?' he asked rhetorically. 'He would enjoy making an arse of a big case like this.'

The two men shared a silent smile. 'That must be our dog walker?' he nodded to towards a soaking Bertie Sweeney being questioned by McGlaughlin. He turned to Mansell, the rain pelting on his angry forehead. 'Can count him out for a start.'

Mansell didn't ask why, just left a suitable gap in the conversation for his boss to jump into.

'He's the manager of the pub I was in last night,' he stated. 'He can maybe fill in a few blanks for *me*.'

Mansell laughed quietly. 'Do you not think it would do you better to give up drinking instead of smoking?'

'And deal with this guff sober?' Steele countered. 'I think not.'

They walked slowly towards the car and both men peered through the windscreen. Amid the flashes from the camera the stunned face of the victim stared dully at them. 'Christ!' Steele sighed. He recognised her. Blond, slim, exceptionally attractive, dressed expensively her diamond necklace sat snugly in the canyon between her breasts, her legs splayed exposing athletic alabaster thighs. If this was where three nights hardcore a week in the gym got you, then you could stick it. Her hair was matted with blood and her throat had been sliced. Breasts exposed crudely, in a manner suggesting it was an afterthought, not part of the original crime, Steele concluded. This didn't appear to be a sex crime, a rape gone wrong? If such a thing wasn't a misnomer.

It was no robbery either, the diamond necklace must have been worth at least three grand. Her head was slumped to one side, the tongue hanging out of her lipstick red mouth had been hacked at coarsely. 'Somebody's tried to cut that off,' he said to Mansell. 'Get these photos done as quickly as you can,' he instructed the photographer. 'There's no need to get into all the artsy fartsy creative angles. Get her done and covered up quick as you can. Don't want this turning into a freakshow.'

'Can't sir,' the photographer answered. 'Still waiting on forensics. DI McGlaughlin's orders sir.'

'No worries,' Steele concluded. 'Maybe pick up something on site rather than transporting everything back to the lab in bags.'

Steele walked across to where McGlaughlin was talking to Bertie. The barman recognised him instantly. 'Jesus! It's yourself, you're a dark one. You told me you were a bloody crossword compiler.'

'In a sense I am,' mused Steele. 'I collect a lot of clues and try to get them to fit. What time did I leave last night?'

Bertie laughed. 'Should it not be you asking me the questions?'

'Fair point,' he turned to McGlaughlin. 'What we got John Number Two?'

McGlaughlin bit his lip before answering in a parrot fashion. 'Mister Sweeney here was walking his dog at approximately six thirty this mo…'

'Enough,' Steele stopped him in his tracks. 'Did you see anybody on your travels Bertie? Anybody at all? That's all we really want to know.'

'No one,' he replied. 'I already told all this to that yoke over there.' he nodded towards a uniformed officer clapping the dog. 'The fecker made *me* feel like a criminal.'

'Not every police officer is as subtle as myself, to some everyone's a potential suspect. That's why I get to wear my own clothes.'

'We've no idea who she is yet,' McGlaughlin interrupted, annoyed that Steele had hijacked the conversation. the system's down at source, can't even get an ID from her number plates. Think it could be a robbery or a lover's tiff gone wrong.'

'Don't be so stupid!' snarled Steele. 'That is no robbery, and if I had just murdered my lover in a fit of peak, the last thing I'd try to do is cut off their tongue just to make matters worse for myself.' Steele shook his head, some rain from his hair hitting off McGlaughlin's face. He pointed back at the car. 'And she, is Georgina McBride. Divorce lawyer extraordinaire. Do you people know nothing.' he turned his attention back to Bertie. 'Mister Sweeney,' he almost laughed at how serious he sounded talking to Bertie. A few hours previously he would have been slurring at him and calling him all sorts. 'Can you keep this quiet? Not the murder, but the state she's in? We don't want every Tom Dick knowing the gory details and rolling up with a confession. Whoever did this is dangerous. Seriously dangerous.'

'No problem, like.' replied Bertie. 'REVEL!' he barked, causing McGlaughlin to flinch. 'C'mere ya flea-bitten mutt ya!'

Steele spotted Mansell staring through the rain at the swings, roundabout and slide in the children's park. He walked over and patted his shoulder. 'You're miles away son, all the action's over there.'

'It's a great spot this,' he said distantly. 'Alice and the girls love having wee picnics up here. I would go on one with them if I wasn't working all the bloody time.'

'Don't think you'll be joining them any time soon.' Steele stated. 'I'd say all leave was about to be cancelled until we catch this nutter.' He guided him back to face the crime scene. 'You get this lot doing a search of the area. Looking for a weapon. Just as far as the eye can see.'

'That's as far as the eye can see,' he said, pointing at the East End of Glasgow.

'You know what I mean,' Steele told him. 'Round and about the car, on the road towards the main road, see if there's anything untoward.'

'Right,' Mansell walked slowly towards the nearest uniformed officer, the rain resting wearily on his shoulders.

A car pulled up behind him, the tyres rasping on the gravel. Another black Audi. Sarinder Kapoor, head of Forensics at the wheel. Seemed to be a new car every other month, mused Steele. Who said crime didn't pay? Kapoor opened his door and swung his legs out, his eyes skyward, not wanting to get his sleek black hair wet. Steele's walk towards him was to the backdrop of an unexpected roar of thunder that made him stop in his tracks.

As he reached the car he saw that Kapoor was on the phone, hands-free, and held up a finger to let him know he wouldn't be a minute. Steele examined his shoes.

'Listen,' Kapoor said, head shaking from side to side. 'Listen, got to go. Got to go. Bye.' He pulled the headset from his ear. 'You are a very lucky man Detective Inspector. No wife asking you why you did this? Why you didn't do that? Why, why, why. The favourite word of a wife. I had no idea I was so wrong about everything until I married her. Oh how I miss the single life.'

'It's not all it's cracked up to be Sarinder,' Steele smiled. 'There's many a day I'm absolutely choking for a bit of nagging. It's the little things you miss,' he added whimsically. He felt the sole of his left foot was wet, and lifted it and looked at the bottom of his shoe. They were on their last legs.

'Have you stood in dog shit?' asked Sarinder with a frown.

'No, no, it's just my shoes.'

Sarinder looked as Steele's shoes and then at his suit. 'You're an old man before your time Detective Inspector Robert Steele.' The forensics man shook his head. 'You like the comfy casual. A man of your age and importance should make more of a statement, be more thrusting. You need a serious makeover, more dynamism. You're more Caledonian Tour than Club 18-30.'

'Cheers for that,' Steele mused. 'You mind if I pop in the passenger side? This rain's not doing my *comfy casual* suit any favours.'

As he sat down Kapoor looked at his trousers and laughed. 'The rain makes it look like you pished yourself old man.'

Steele looked and couldn't help but agree, but rubbed at his thighs to slosh away the worst of it.

'So,' Kapoor began. 'A female? Anything else?'

'I've just had a quick look,' answered Steele. 'Battered about the head, we can tell that. Her throat's been cut.' he paused. 'And he's tried to hack her tongue off. Don't know what that's about.'

Kapoor frowned. 'Sounds more premeditated than a crime of passion – lust gone awry. Sexual?'

Steele laughed. 'How would I know? I think it was the eighties the last time I got a bit.'

Kapoor rolled his eyes. 'We need a makeover on your personality as well Robert Steele. You are a fine man, a good catch.'

'Are you trying for a new career in stand up?' smiled Steele.

'I could set you up,' Kapoor winked. 'I have many friends. Hunners.'

Steele smiled at the inelegance of the vernacular sullying his normally eloquent mouth. 'Funnily enough,' he paused again. 'She's... She *was* a divorce lawyer. One of the dirtiest, think she's the one that shafted the Chief Super.'

'Oh aye,' Kapoor raised an eyebrow.

'In the courts,' Steele added. 'Wife took him to the cleaners and left him standing in just his vest and skiddies.'

'Not a pleasant image you have implanted in my head.'

'Certainly is not. Hopefully there's plenty of prints and evidence in the car to get this wrapped up as quickly as possible.'

'Right,' Steele opened his door. 'I've got to go and break the news to the nearest and dearest.'

'Wouldn't want to be in your shoes for that. Literally. See you back at the ranch Detective Inspector.'

'Cheers Sarinder.' Steele closed the door over and looked around for Mansell. He was staring blankly at the windscreen, at the dead lawyer. He looked like a little lost boy. Steele hollered at him to come over.

'Bad business sir,' he said quietly.

'And it's going to get worse. We're on nearest and dearest duties.'

'Oh sir, can we not get...'

'Get in the car and drive.' Steele instructed. 'I'd rather do it subtly than have some monkey blurt it out to them.' He looked over to McGlaughlin and shook his head.

As the car was parallel with the yellow art deco building on the Lugton Road Steele caught sight of Bertie and his dog up ahead. 'Stop and give the Big Fella a lift,' he said to Mansell.

Mansell reluctantly pulled up beside Bertie and Steele shouted through the open window. 'Get in Bertie!'

Bertie leaned towards the window. 'You're all right lads,' he looked down at his clothes. 'I'm drenched.'

'Get in. I insist,' Steele told him.

He insists? Mansell thought. Never mind the upholstery with his soaking clothes and mutt.

Bertie got in the back of the car. 'It's Bardrain Road,' he said. 'Just up from St Peter's chapel.'

Mansell wondered where he had misplaced the taxi meter for his car. 'No problem.' The smell of wet dog? Marvellous.

3

The area of Ralston sat to the east of Paisley town centre and positively reeked of old money. Georgina McBride (nee Smyth) had grown up in Ralston and always did what was expected of her. After shining at The Grammar and Glasgow University she got her first job with Spottiswood, Harris and Wishart, one of the longest established law firms in the burgh. She had known the three partners all her life, they were golfing buddies of her father, a GP with his own practice on the Glasgow Road. After three years learning the ropes she set up on her own, specialising in family and divorce matters. Aged twenty-five, she married the golf pro at her father's club, Finlay McBride. Ten years and no children later, she was dead in the car park in the sky, battered about the head, her throat sliced and her tongue hacked at.

Steele rapped aggressively on the front door of the detached house that the now up and running system told him Georgina McBride had shared with her husband Finlay for the last ten years. As he was about to hit the door for a second time Mansell pointed out a bell to him.

'Like a bull in a china shop,' he muttered audibly.

Steele lifted his eyebrows to him before pointing a finger towards the bell. Before he had a chance to ring it a figure appeared through the mottled glass. The door opened and Finlay McBride stood before them in all his splendour, dressed in a silk red dressing gown that barely reached his thighs.

'Yes?' he eyed the two men blearily.

'Finlay McBride?' asked Steele.

'Clearly,' McBride pointed to the nameplate on the door.

Steele held up his ID for McBride to see and indicated for Mansell to do the same. 'Police. Could we come in please?'

The expression on McBride's face changed from weary arrogance to helpless fear. 'Well, it's not really a good time at the moment. Whatever you need to know we can sort it out here,' he grabbed hold of the edge of the door and moved it forward slightly as though blocking their entry.

'It really would be better if we came in sir,' Mansell pleaded. 'We have some bad news.'

McBride was adamant however. 'You can tell me here. I'm a big boy I can take it.'

'We think you'd rather it was in...' Mansell started.

'Just tell me the news and we can all get on...'

'Your wife Georgina McBride has been murdered,' Steele said firmly. 'She's been battered and had her throat cut in what looks like a frenzied attack.'

McBride held on to the door more firmly, not to block anyone's entrance, but for balance, the inside of his head had just gone totally blank and his heart was pumping at an industrial rate. He lost consciousness and fell backwards onto the wooden flooring, exposing his genitals as he lay prone. 'He was right about being a big boy,' Steele's eyes widened. 'That's some mashie niblick.' He leant in and closer inspected McBride's meat and two. 'What's that Mansell?'

Mansell shook his head; his bosses lack of subtlety had just plumbed new depths. 'Cock ring, sir.' He answered unenthusiastically.

Steele screwed up his face and shook his head. 'I think we should maybe try and lift him through to the sitting room.' The two men took an arm each and dragged the groggy golf pro through to his living room. He came round just as they sat him on the leather couch.

'I can see now why he didn't want us coming in,' Mansell eyed the coffee table, two lines of white powder, visible among the magazines and clutter strewn over it.

'Let's just pretend we never saw it, eh?' Steele stared at his colleague. 'Mr McBride here has more pressing things on at the minute. No buts Mansell,' he said, just as his colleague's mouth was pursed to speak. Mansell's eyes relented.

'What...What...What...' McBride's eyes were everywhere, his head shaking involuntarily.

Steele sat down opposite, and was instantly sorry he did so. The golf pro's tackle was dangling for all to see, swinging like a pendulum. 'Sorry about breaking the news to you on the doorstep Mr McBride, but we had no choice.' He coughed. 'We don't care about the stuff on the coffee table there, we just need to talk to you about your wife Georgina.' he paused. He'd broken this kind of news countless times and always felt it important to allow the recently bereaved the chance to talk as much as possible. It was also amazing how many clues and confessions people blurted out.

McBride buried his face in his hands and Steele wished he would cover up his cock. He just couldn't keep his eyes off it. 'You said,' McBride spluttered. 'You said she had been battered and had her throat cut? That's...that's unbelievable.'

'Were you not surprised when she didn't come home last night sir?' Mansell asked.

Steele threw him a look that told him this was no time for any *good cop bad cop* routine he might have picked up off the TV.

McBride rubbed at his hair. 'Eh, no, no. Georgie and I we're...' he exhaled heavily. 'We're separated, she moved out.'

'When was this sir,' Mansell asked.

'Over six months ago,' McBride replied. 'Just after her mum died. February, she moved into one of her work flats next to Brodie Park.'

'The address?'

'Eh, Fourteen G, Viewpoint Gardens. Why is this...why is this important? Should you not be trying to find whoever killed her? Why would anybody want to ki...' his voice trailed and his head dropped into his hands. He started crying uncontrollably. He leant back on the couch and let out an almighty shriek. Steele and Mansell both looked at each other with sympathetic eyes. They were either showing empathy towards the man or didn't want to catch sight of his mammoth organ again.

'We have to find out what her life was like Finlay,' Steele spoke, but his words were falling on deaf ears. 'So that we can eliminate some things and...' he didn't see any point in continuing. Over the sobbing he heard a pair of what sounded like elephant feet on the stairs. A voice shouting.

'Fin! What is it Fin? What's the...' Six foot two of tanned moustachioed Muscle Mary stood in the doorway staring at them. He wore the same flimsy robe. 'Who the fuck are you pair?' he moved forward with purpose.

'It's the police,' McBride spluttered. 'It's Georgie.'

The man walked towards McBride. 'What's that cow been up to now?'

'She's been murdered sir,' Steele told him coldly.

'Oh Jesus!' His face blanched and he slumped down next to McBride on the sofa and once more Steele and Mansell groaned and averted their eyes. Flashed in stereo. 'I'm sorry.' He rubbed McBride's shoulder. 'Are you okay?'

Steele noticed that Mansell had taken out his notebook and was pulling the pen from the centre spine of it. He nodded for him to continue with the questioning.

'Can I ask who you are sir?'

'John McCabe,' he answered immediately. 'Fin's partner.'

'I hope you don't mind me asking these questions sir,' Mansell wrote in his notebook. 'As my colleague was just saying we have to try and establish who would want to do this to Mrs McBride. We also need to eliminate anyone else, such as yourself and Mr. McBride, from our investigations.'

Steele admired his technique, tell them he thinks they're innocent, get them relaxed. Relaxed suspects talk more, tell more tales, admit to misdemeanours. 'Can I ask when you last saw your wife?' Mansell was trying hard not to sound judgemental, he had to say "wife", the "deceased", the "victim" etc. all sounded too clinical, too cold.

'A few weeks ago,' McBride shook his head as though dislodging a false memory. 'Maybe a month. She was up at the golf club for a function.'

'Can you think of any enemies she may have had?'

'She was a lawyer!' McBride answered incredulously. 'Right up there with traffic wardens and tax inspectors.'

'And police,' added Steele with a wry smile. 'Thought I would say it before you did.'

'No one specific though?' asked Mansell.

'None that spring instantly to mind.'

'Do you mind me asking how she was with regard to you John?' Steele interjected.

'Loved me like a brother,' McCabe answered dryly.

'She's dead sir,' sighed Steele. 'Please don't be more obstructive than is necessary.'

'Sorry,' he said. 'I don't know, we never really knew each other, other than through Fin. Stuff to do with the divorce and that. She wasn't bitter or anything.'

'Everything was very straightforward with Georgie,' McBride interrupted. 'I think the word is pragmatic. Things happened, she got on with it, didn't mope about, just moved on. She didn't seem to resent John, if that's what you're implying.'

Steele exhaled with a puffing sound. 'Right at the moment we don't know what we're implying. Our investigation is at a very early stage and we're looking for all the information we can get. We do have to ask you about your whereabouts last night. We don't have a specific timeframe at present though.'

The two men rattled off the names of half a dozen pubs in Glasgow, none of which rang any bells with Steele, and all of which Mansell dutifully noted down, even though they both knew they had no intention of checking any one of them. They had arrived home about two and had carried on their party at home until they had fallen into bed at half three.

'We may need you to formally identify the body.' Steele added as he and Mansell got to their feet. 'Will that be alright?'

'Fine.' McBride answered, as at last he and John got to their feet and stopped flashing the policemen.

Mansell made a note of their mobile numbers as Steele let himself out.

He pulled up his collar as he made the short walk to the car, the rain still hammering down. Less than a minute later Mansell joined him. 'Don't know about you,' he smiled. 'But that gave me the willies.'

'It's put me right off the notion of a sausage sandwich for a kick off.'

Mansell started the car and they headed back towards the town centre, giggling like schoolboys.

Viewpoint Gardens, on the cusp of Brodie Park, had some of the most panoramic vistas Paisley had to offer, the fourth floor, where apartment G was sited was no exception. On a clear day it offered a view of Ben Lomond and the Old Kilpatrick Hills to the north, and as far as East Kilbride to the south. Today was not a clear day, driech at best. Through the impressively large windows all that could be seen was patches of darkness and impending funnels of rain. Night was closing in, and it wasn't even lunchtime. The concierge had let them in, a man in his early sixties sporting black flannels, a beige cardigan and a pair of ten pound supermarket shoes. He had introduced himself in the foyer as McKenzie. He had then laughed and said it was his first name, his full name was McKenzie Alexander. Steele had induced his ire by asking if that was his middle name and the pedantic swine had closely inspected their warrant cards, scrutinising them through bottle top glasses that were tied round his neck with a fading brown bootlace. He had asked about a warrant but Mansell had placated him with buzz words like "Sunday", "Judges sleeping or on holiday" and the crème de la crème, "murder investigation". The concierge had almost soiled his flannels when that one had been pulled out the bag.

Now the concierge was pacing up and down in the living room of Georgina McBride's anodyne flat, muttering to himself. He carried a broom handle marked with red pen in his hand. Steele squinted to see what it said "do not remove from office!!!". He could imagine the other concierges, if there were any, seeing this old duffer as an invaluable and never ending source of entertainment.

'What's the pole for?' Steele asked, causing McKenzie Alexander to stop in his tracks.

He chomped a bit before he spoke, as though swallowing excess saliva. 'Warden calls,' he beamed. With the pole held aloft he walked to the smoke alarm and prodded it meticulously.

The alarm beeped loudly for ten seconds much to Steele's annoyance. 'You do this every Sunday?'

'Religiously,' Alexander laughed again unnecessarily. 'Just the communal areas.'

'The Sunday morning hangover crew must love you,' Steele shook his head to get the ringing from his ears.

'I'm sure they'd rather that than be found dead in their bed for want of a missed warden call.'

Steele muttered under his breath, he wasn't so sure. 'If you want to carry on with them we don't need you to be here, we'll drop the key at the front desk.'

'You don't mind?'

'Not at all,' Steele shooed him towards the door. 'Don't want the good people of Viewpoint Gardens dying in their beds now, do we?'

Alexander left and shut the door awkwardly behind him, almost catching a leg in it. All the while he laughed to himself like an idiot. 'Thank Christ for that,' Steele said to Mansell. 'Imagine working with *that* every day?'

'At least you wouldn't die in your bed,' laughed Mansell. 'What do you think?' Mansell looked around the living room, minimalist wasn't even close. Two settees facing each other on some oak wooden flooring, no mirrors, photographs or paintings on the walls, just a TV and an empty bookshelf.

'It looks like what it is,' Steele started. 'A crash pad for folk that work in an office and can't make it home'

'But she was here for six months?'

'Maybe she didn't like clutter,' Steele suggested.

'But there's not even a magazine or a book?'

'It's temporary,' Steele answered. 'You go to a hotel for two weeks, you don't start sticking up pictures of the wife and kids, do you?'

'No but... Six months?'

'Personally, I'm impressed by the lack of clutter.' Steele could feel last nights' alcohol still in his system, at his babble gland. 'Shows an ordered mind, a person who knows exactly where she is, in limbo. She knew she was just passing through this apartment and didn't want the emotional upheaval of packing up sentimental curios when at last it came time to move.' Steele nodded, he had made it all up on the spot, nonsense, but nonsense that made some sort of sense to him.

'You don't half talk some pish sir,' Mansell replied. 'Bedroom?'

'Dave, I never knew you cared.' Steele minced towards the bedroom door. When there he pulled across the mirrored ceiling to floor wardrobes and examined their contents. A wardrobe for work clothes – mostly black trousers and skirts and white blouses, a wardrobe filled with sparkling cocktail dresses and finally one filled with casual wear. Steele noticed something hidden at the back of the wardrobe containing the work wear though and pulled it out. 'What do you make of this Dave?' he asked Mansell as he entered the room.

Mansell squinted at the mini tartan skirt Steele held by the hanger and raised a weary eyebrow. 'I certainly don't remember Fran and Anna wearing anything that revealing when they were at their peak.'

Steele shook his head and placed the skirt back in the wardrobe, discarding it from his thoughts. 'Probably fancy dress or something.'

'As far as I can see this is a dead end, unless,' Steele let a mischievous smile cross his dry lips.

'No,' Mansell scowled, 'whatever it is. No!'

'You're no fun anymore Dave Mansell,' pouted Steele. 'We could wind up that janitor guy, with the pole. Take his broom handle into custody, tell him it's for forensic checks. What do you say?'

'No.' Mansell shook his head. 'In case you've forgotten, this is a murder enquiry. We don't have time to fanny about with practical jokes.'

Steele felt instantly chastened, confirming his status as still being a wee bitty pished from the previous night. 'Righty ho, let's go then son. There's nothing here. It's bank details, clients, friends and family I'm afraid. The jumped up jannie's off the hook.'

They left the building without seeing the concierge, or his pole.

4

As he made his approach to the stadium Harry Spencer cursed the soaking predictability of the Scottish weather. He had been planning for this day all through the closed season. In his daydreams he had imagined it to be a blister bursting scorcher of a day, but cometh the hour, cometh the biblical downpour. He had slept fitfully, eventually getting up at seven, desperate to check that the paint on his latest banner had dried. His planning was getting better, he hadn't eaten or drank anything, because he knew he was going to be on the roof of the stadium a long time, and didn't want to be dragged down before the cameras arrived with anything running down his leg other than rainwater. He had no need to encourage the local paper any further. They were already out to get him.

His two embarrassing brushes with The Paisley Daily Express had made him look like an absolute clown – nothing like the caring father he had wanted to come across as. The hapless nature of his previous attempts to have his grievance further investigated had caused them to change his first name to "Frank", and adding insult to this, they had photo-shopped a snap of him wearing a beret and having a cartoon bubble appearing from his mouth with the caption "Ooh Betty!" inside it.

His first attempt to draw attention to his plight, in true west of Scotland fashion, had been a drunken escapade. Giro day, the consumption of too strong lager and cheap doubles at a solo session in The Last Post, caused him to resemble a firework at one second to midnight on November the fourth. He was bursting to explode at the injustice of his situation. He didn't normally throw all his giro money behind a bar, but this particular Monday he had received a rejection letter from the protest group Fathers For Justice, explaining coldly that his plight was not something that they wished their organisation to be associated with. In the pub he was just another rambling, shambling drunk with a case of the "poor me's", so he decided to take his fight outside, where the people wouldn't be expecting it, and may therefore be more responsive.

The war memorial that stood proudly at the junction of The High Street and Gilmour Street had seen better days, the three infantry men and the rider on the charger that stood twenty foot on top of the concrete plinth, looking more like they had been fighting the pigeons than the Germans. They were coated from helmet to boot in bird shit. The three council workers who had been taking it in turns to climb the scaffold and point their shared power washer at the memorial were round at Greggs in Moss Street, leaving Harry with the perfect opportunity to shout his case from horseback. There had been a few wobbles on the way up the scaffold, and he felt physically sick as he mounted the horse, his arms clasped round the iron rider's stomach for balance. He hadn't realised how high up it would be. As usual the crowd that congregated below on the concrete steps were a desolate band of junkies, jakies, track-suited neds and Goths holding skateboards they should have grown out of years ago. One of the neds had spotted him just as he had clambered to the top of the plinth and began instantly berating him. Once the rest of the gathered mass saw what he had been shouting at they all looked to the skies and demanded that Harry Spencer entertain them.

Truth be told, he was terrified, too scared to say anything at first, but after a couple of seconds of coughing and clearing his throat he was ready to tell them a story. He shouted down to them how he couldn't get access to his "Little Buffalo Soldier" Marley, how his mother was denying him any contact, had taken out a restraining order since their split. Didn't we all have equal right? Where were the rights for the father? He omitted to tell them the most important thing though – the fact that he wasn't the father of his "Little Buffalo Soldier". A glaring omission, but he felt it might prejudice the crowd against him. He ranted incoherently about the injustice of the divorce system and the way lawyers were getting rich off the back of people's misery. Again, he failed to inform the crowd that he hadn't been married.

Harry Spencer had been dumped by a single mother after a six-month relationship and it had torn his heart out. Angie, the mother, was not the reason for the almost palpable pain he felt in his heart. That was down to her son Marley. At thirty-nine Harry Spencer had never felt like a father, but he did to this little three-year-old. He'd had to, Angie was a disaster, more concerned with getting high than taking Marley to the park, playing with him and his toys, his teddy's, just generally paying him any attention at all. To Angie, Marley was an inconvenience, a reminder of something she really knew nothing about. A stoned tryst in Amsterdam with a man whose name she couldn't remember. High on the horse in the sky Harry Spencer had run out of things to say and could feel tears welling up inside. Down below the crowd were bored – just another incoherent shambles of a man with mental health issues - and began throwing chips and cans at him. This caught the eagle-eyes of some bottom-feeding birds, gulls mostly, and they began dive bombing the war memorial with all the precision of the Luftwaffe over Clydebank. It only took two or three swoops from the birds for Harry Spencer to lose his balance and fall from his horse. As he bounced onto the wood of the scaffold he tried to find something to hold onto, but all he could do was think of the words to "Two Little Boys". His momentum kept him rolling and in desperation he clutched at the corner of two adjoined bars with his right hand, the rest of his body swung precariously in the air. Thankfully the birds had decided to seek out other prey and the crowd had reverted to taking collective intakes of breath instead of throwing things at him. He swung like a monkey, a drunken monkey, for about five seconds before losing his grip and falling to the rock hard ground, just beside the returning council workers. Remarkably he sustained just a sprained ankle and some cuts and bruises. Nothing serious. The Express picked up on the story- it merited two hundred words on the right hand corner of page eight, and said nothing of his reasons, just his descent and his idiotic and callous behaviour.

Things would be different on the second occasion. He was sure of that. After eight days of stewing Harry Spencer and his sprained ankle were back to full fitness and had devised his plan soberly. It involved theft and trespass, but he was sure it would be worth it, he would at last get his point across and be looked upon sympathetically by the burghers of Paisley, and then perhaps, get a bit of access to Marley.

He had stolen an old blue SOMERFIELD banner from the railings of the taxi rank in County Square. He felt he was doing the town a favour, the shop in the Piazza had long been taken over by the Co-op, and the banner was simply a piece of leftover litter. He had painted **JUSTICE FOR HARRY SPENCER!** on the reverse of it. This would surely get people talking – "Who was Harry Spencer?" "What was his grievance?" All without mentioning Angie or Marley, for he knew that would only hinder his cause, and there would be the chance that she would get that man-hating lawyer onto him again. The woman had terrified him, she was a pitbull. He had also committed another theft, one that could earn him a kicking. He had stolen a set of ladders from the roof of the van of one of his neighbours in the close – a giant of a man with a window cleaning round.

At seven o'clock on Saturday morning he phoned the office of The Paisley Daily Express to tell them what he was about to do but all he got was an automated message from an answer phone. He left a message detailing his name, what he was about to do as well as the time and the date. He then walked through the West End towards the town centre carrying his stolen ladder on one shoulder and banner in a holdall on the other. He had to keep swapping around every thirty feet or so, the ladder was a lot heavier than it looked. The wind was whistling through the rungs causing a ringing in his ears.

He eventually made the St James bridge, and stretched the ladder over the rail and propped it against the south facing wall of the town hall. He climbed gingerly towards the nearest ledge. The ledge, although covered in spikes to deter birds from landing on it, held no fears for him. He had industrial strength wire cutters which lived up to their billing and before long he was stood on the ledge and shimmying round to the small balcony on the west facing wall. The balcony hadn't been used in years, and was decaying and yellow, but safe enough, he assured himself, bouncing slightly and feeling no wobbles underfoot. He took his banner from his holdall and fastened the tie ropes of one end of it to the first column on the balcony. The wind caught it instantly and it began flapping and twisting around snake-like, taking on a life of its own, the free rope ties hitting him on the forehead before he finally grabbed a hold of the bulk of the banner. As he began to unwind it he heard a clatter to his left and guessed the ladder had been caught by the same fearsome blast of wind. He steadied himself, noting that his centre of gravity was higher than that of the balcony, eyeing the choppy waters of the White Cart below with some trepidation. Even though he was only about thirty feet above the water level he felt the wind had substantially increased and decided to take some remedial action. He twisted the remaining ropes around his wrist before gingerly making his way along the length of the balcony to the far corner. The middle of the banner caught a huge gust of wind and twisted like a spinning top. He tried to unravel it by flapping his wrist like a trapped bird. This had a negative effect on his balance and he soon found himself on the other side of the balcony heading for the White Cart. Luckily, he was quick to react and his free hand grabbed at one of the vertical pillars of the balcony. He managed to get his forearm around the pillar, but much as he tried he just didn't have the strength to lift either leg and get back on the balcony to safety. He was no Indiana Jones. He tried to cry for help, but his voice was weak. Managing to breathe properly was about as much as he could do. He heard the noise of a couple of buses to the side of him, but was too afraid to turn. Thankfully one of the drivers called The Fire Brigade. Before they rescued him with their ladders however, some of them couldn't help but break the rules and take a photo of the dangling Harry Spencer with their mobiles.

The image of him on the front page of The Express still haunted him. There he was hanging precariously and looking terrified, all the while clinging to a twisted banner that spelt out the word **A**R**SE**H**O**L**E!** He was the new laughing stock of Paisley.

This time it would be different however, even this driving rain wouldn't stop his driving ambition. He scaled the fence of St Mirren Park on Greenfields Road and made his way over to the home stand. This was a lot easier than he thought it was going to be. Where was the security?

5

'I don't care,' Steele remarked to the kitchen supervisor, 'deep cleaning or no deep cleaning, I'm willing to take my chances.'

'No can do,' she shook her head. 'We need to have the kitchen shut. We thought Sunday would be a quiet day. It normally is.'

'Normally, but we've got a murder enquiry and a lot of hungry officers. None of the wee cafes in town are open, what are we meant to do?'

'McDonalds?' she suggested.

'I'll pretend I never heard that.' Steele needed his bacon fix, but could sense the situation was hopeless. He tried one last time. 'What if we bought the stuff in? Could we cook it ourselves?'

'No chance.' The kitchen supervisor crossed her arms, case closed. Steele knew that it didn't matter how high up the greasy pole you climbed, there would always be some people in the station over whom you had no power. He sarcastically thanked her for her time and turned on his heels toward the back stairwell – the lifts were being serviced as well – and his third floor office. He sat behind his desk and stared out of his window without a view. His office was directly opposite the newly re-furbished council buildings, no matter how they dressed them up architecturally, they were still drab, grey and faceless – a bit like their inhabitants. The council buildings had long been referred to as "La La Land!" by those in Paisley not too inebriated by drink or drugs to notice, and on a daily basis Steele could see why. From his vantage point he could see lots of "workspaces" but very rarely any sign of activity, except on a Friday when some sort of weekend sweepstake caught the attention of the inhabitants, causing them to chatter and scurry like drunken ants – it was the sort of place, Steele surmised, where some overweight lassie went round in May organising the Christmas night out. Nightmare! His daydream was interrupted by the ring of the telephone.

He picked up the receiver on the second ring. 'Steele! Speak,' he instructed.

'Charmed, I am sure DI Robert Steele,' Kapoor informed him. 'You have the telephone manner of a peasant. This is the digital age and...'

And, Steele didn't let him finish. 'and in that it is the digital age, what have you got for me?'

'Hee Haw!' Sarinder Kapoor laughed, another Scottish expression tickling his tonsils. 'This fellow does not have a record. No DNA, nothing. I can't help but say I am very disappointed.'

'You're not the only one,' sighed Steele.

'But we can tell you he has blond hair, he...'

'Blondie what you fondae?' Steele muttered, not realising he was speaking out loud.

'Yes,' Kapoor continued, 'blond hair, type O blood, probably a lot of scratches over him and possibly a mark from where he had been kicked by the lady lawyer's high heel. We have many fingerprints. The lab said she struggled terribly. So, bruise marks on her arms and inside her legs.'

'Anything sexual?' Steele asked, the words sticking in his craw as Kapoor answered jovially.

'She was ploutered in every orifice, barring her eyes and ears,' he laughed. 'But we haven't checked them thoroughly yet. This woman lawyer was very, very sexually active before she died.'

'So, are we looking at rape as well?' Steele opened the drawer to his desk, even though he knew he had banished every cigarette from his life.

'I do not think so.' Kapoor answered. 'There are no signs of struggle in those areas of her body,' he paused slightly. 'Apart from her mouth of course.'

Steele had no option other than to think about Georgina McBride's heavily lip-sticked lips wrapping themselves around a cock. 'Anything else,' he sighed.

'These are just preliminaries,' Sarinder told him. 'We have yet to cut her open.'

'Too much information.' Steele baulked. 'What about the knife that cut her tongue?'

'Common or garden kitchen knife. Serrated edge. See them in every supermarket. *To you sir, five ninety-nine*, ha ha.' Kapoor laughed at his market seller Asian repartee.

Steele was about to say his goodbyes when a thought struck him. 'Sarinder. Do you have a microwave in your lab by any chance?'

Seconds later Steele sent a disgruntled Mansell out on an errand of mercy. To hunt down as much bacon as he could carry and a dozen crusty rolls. 'An army marches on its' stomach after all.'

Twenty-five minutes later Mansell slammed two packets of Danish bacon on Steele's desk and placed the two bags of morning rolls beside them. 'There you go boss,' he said, sullenly. 'Might I ask where you intend to cook this bacon?'

'In the lab,' he informed Mansell. 'They've got a microwave.'

'The lab!' Mansell barked. 'You don't know what's been in there! Jesus! Count me out, I'd rather go hungry.'

'I am very much counting you in my dear boy,' Steele handed him back the packets of bacon. 'Get them down there, Sarinder's waiting on them, and I don't mean for examination.'

'Come on,' Mansell pleaded. 'There must be…' Saved by the bell.

Steele picked it up the receiver on the second ring. 'Speak!'

Whoever was on the other end of the telephone seemed to do just that. They spoke and Steele listened and sighed heavily, listened and sighed. Mansell stood, bacon in hand, waiting for him to come off the phone – this could be some sort of reprieve from batch-cooking bacon in a laboratory microwave. He had eaten some mind-boggling things in his student days, but the thought of this turned his stomach. Steele put down the receiver and sighed once more.

'Trouble?' asked Mansell.

'Something like that,' Steele grabbed the bacon from him and put it in his desk drawer. 'You and I are going to St. Mirren Park.'

'Why?'

'It appears someone has broken into the stadium and is all set on making a protest.'

'But why?' Mansell asked rhetorically. 'The game's at...'

'I know son,' Steele informed him. 'The game's at Parkhead, eight miles in that direction.' Steele pointed at the door, unsure whether his compass-pointing finger was accurate or not.

'What are they protesting...'

'It's that idiot Spencer again, demanding rights that he just isn't entitled to.'

'How so sir?'

'How so!' Steele screeched incredulously, grabbing his linen jacket from the back of the chair. 'Have you bothered to find out what he's protesting about?'

'He wants access to his child,' Mansell replied. 'I think that's fairly understandable, he may not be going about it in the right way but...'

'But!' Steele held a finger in the air then opened the door. 'But, the child he is seeking access to *is* not his, its' DNA belongs to some random from over three years ago.'

'Yeah, but, I suppose he feels some sort of connection with the...'

'The mother is white, Spencer is white, the boy is black.' Steele shook his head as they made it to the top of the stairs. 'It's not that I care, but Spencer's making a monumental tit out of himself. I mean, who's going to take him seriously? He was only with the mother for about two months! Just long enough for the social to sort out the benefits and then she papped him out on his idiotic jacksy.'

'I didn't know any of this,' Mansell gulped. 'Certainly seems strange that he's got such a bee in his bonnet about it.'

'Do none of you people read the local papers?' Steele opened the passenger side door. 'Where else are you going to find out who all the bad guys and gals are?'

'Sorry?' Mansell didn't know what he was getting at. They had reached his car.

'The local paper has made him a laughing stock, not even deliberately. All they did was state the facts of the case.' Steele lowered his window slightly to rid the car of some of its condensation. 'Obviously they put a wee bit of slant on it, but not much. The guy's now one of the best known arseholes this burgh's ever produced.'

'It is a bit sad though sir,' Mansell suggested, starting the engine.

'It isn't sad Mansell,' he told him bluntly. 'It's a mental health problem. He's just one of the many walking about out there undiagnosed.' Steele waved his hand at the windscreen. 'There are thousands of the buggers, all walking about talking to themselves and telling any poor sod unfortunate enough to listen how life isn't fair and that it's always someone else's fault. Usually the social. They want rounded up and shot.' Steele said calmly. 'Greenhills Road driver,' he laughed.

They arrived at the stadium where a disgruntled and decrepit pensioner of a groundsman checked their ID before letting them in. The old man grunted twice, once at each ID. He had the look of someone who would burst balloons at the birthday party of a terminally ill child.

'Shame you couldn't have been as conscientious earlier on,' Steele scowled at the jobsworth as they walked down the tunnel and onto the park. 'Seems you'd let in any Tom, Dick or E-v-e-l K-n-e-i-v-e-l!' Steele said the last name in slow motion, his eyes staring at the figure on the tin roof of the home stand. Harry Spencer, dressed in the famous star-spangled white jump suit of the deceased daredevil, was standing proudly, his banner unfurled and hanging like a ceremonial flag over the side of the roof.

'Everything perfect this time apart from the location,' Mansell laughed.

'He can't stay here,' the disgruntled groundsman scowled at them. 'It's no laughing matter.'

The two policemen turned their heads and threw him a derisory look. 'Why?' Steele asked. 'What's happening here? There's not a game here for another week.'

'Six days actually,' The groundsman corrected him. 'Kilmarnock. Big game, could be a six-pointer come the end of the season.'

Both men again looked at him, this time quizzically. 'But it's not even the start of the sea...' Mansell began, but Steele waved him down. From experience he knew how to silence a pedant. Ignore him. He instructed Mansell to follow him, and stepped on to the pitch.

'Hey you pair! Get off that grass!' the pedant shouted after them. 'You can't go standing on the pitch. This place has to be perfect...' His voice trailed behind them as Steele and Mansell continued walking to the left and Harry Spencer and his rooftop protest.

On the red ash running track behind the goal they were met by one of the community cops.

'Okay McCauley,' Steele eyed him. 'What's so urgent you needed to call in the big boys?'

McCauley smirked and pointed skyward. 'We tried talking him down, but he says he's only willing to negotiate with you.'

'What's he after? A getaway car and a jet to Panama?' Steele shook his head. 'This is getting ridiculous. More and more we're having to deal with this sort of stuff – care in the community policing. This crap is taking up too much of our time, if this was in the states we could just shoot him down and plant something on him later.'

'Like what boss? A fiddle?' Mansell giggled. 'You know, fiddler on the roof...'

'Button it Mansell,' Steele snarled. 'Why me?' he asked McCauley.

'He says you listened to him the last time, you told him things would get sorted out,' McCauley answered.

'Aye,' sighed Steele. 'But Dykebar was full. He doesn't need a sympathetic ear he wants either locking up or a good shag to get all this nonsense out his system.'

'That's not what you were saying to him the last time sir,' Mansell whispered slightly. 'It was all "life's not fair" and "women were a different species" stuff, if you don't mind me saying.' Mansell gulped internally, unsure whether he had crossed the line.

Steele grabbed him playfully by the collar of his raincoat and breathed heavily in his ear. 'I was drunk then; I was happy then. Now, I'm hungover, hungry and hacked off.' He let go of Mansell's collar and clapped his hands together. 'Now, let's get this numpty down off the roof. You!' he shouted at the groundsman, who was now nearing them after walking round the red ash running track. 'Have you got access to the tannoy?'

The guy didn't answer, just scowled and kept walking towards them.

Not to be put off, Steele mouthed the words at him again in silence, causing the guy's eyes to screw up. He carried on walking towards them, cursing the pelting rain for taking away what was left of his hearing. 'Eh?' he asked Steele as he got close to him.

'HAVE YOU GOT ACCESS TO THE TANNOY?' Steele bawled, causing the guy to stumble backwards almost to the point of falling over.

'You big bloody idiot!' The guy shook his head like he was in some silent film. 'You could have deafened me there.'

'Well?' Steele lurched forward. 'Do you? Because he'll never hear me above this din.' In the past minute the rain had got much heavier, the sound of each droplet on the tin roof echoing dramatically through the empty stadium.

'No!' The groundsman barked back, determined to be as unhelpful as possible.

Steele rolled his eyes and cupped his hands round his mouth. He began shouting up at Spencer. Spencer began shouting back down at him, his daredevil costume and cape no real deterrent against the lashing rain, but neither man could hear the other. 'This is hopeless,' Steele told Mansell and McCauley. 'Let's get inside.' The three officers began squelching back across the pitch to the tunnel and the dryness within. The groundsman shouted after them but his voice was lost in the rain and he began traipsing towards the tunnel using the red gravel running track.

In the tunnel the three men wiped themselves down, trying to get the worst of the rain from their clothes. Steele ran his hands down his chest and thighs, the water reluctant to leave his linen suit. Mansell flapped his raincoat like a flasher and shook his head vigorously. McCauley, dressed only in cycling shorts and a figure-hugging top, took off the top and wrung it out. Steele and Mansell stood like small boys in the showers, their heads facing downwards in awe of the constable's remarkable physique.

Steele spoke as he was pulling the wet top over his head. 'You're a show off bugger McCauley. You don't get that kind of figure just peddling a bike all day, you must be on steroids. Remind me to get him drug tested when we get back to Mill Street Mansell.'

'Will do sir,' Mansell joined in, taking out his notebook and pretending to write, his tongue hanging out the side of his mouth. 'Get-McCauley-drug-tested-back-at-the-station,' he said slowly.

'No chance sir,' McCauley boasted. 'There's no muck goes into this body, no toxins or poisons.'

'Sure thing Methusala,' Steele snarled, 'You'll probably live forever.'

'You know,' Mansell began, 'You could get yourself pneumonia putting that wet top straight back on again.' He informed McCauley.

'Double pneumonia,' Steele added – the two out-of-condition males determined to get their jibe in at the fitness freak. 'And that's the worst kind.'

'Thanks for that ladies,' McCauley started, forgetting for a second that he was addressing senior officers. 'You wont mind if I take my shorts off and hang them over a radiator then?'

Both men took a sharp intake of breath. It was Steele who spoke first, 'After the morning we've had, no chance.'

'Think we've seen enough of that for one day, eh sir?' Mansell said.

Lines immediately crossed McCauley's forehead, and question marks fired from his eyes.

'You don't want to know,' Steele told him.

'On the contrary sir,' McCauley's gaze went from Steele to Mansell then back again. 'I think I do.'

'You don't.' Steele told him.

'DON'T,' puffed the groundsman. 'Don't think you can just wait in here till the rain goes off. I need him down out of that roof as soon as...' He was interrupted by a loud, sustained rapping on the Player's entrance door. 'Who the hell's that now,' he juddered towards the door, his whole being resembling one large disgruntled TUT.

'How are we going to get him down sir?' asked Mansell.

McCauley responded before Steele could answer. 'Don Black's away to the builder's yard across the way to try and borrow a big enough ladder. I told him it's normally shut on a Sunday but he was having none of it.'

'I was wondering where your boyfriend was,' Steele chided him. 'Not like you not to be riding tandem.'

'With all due respect sir,' McCauley's voice took on a serious tone, 'don't say anything like that when he gets back. He's having trouble at home and anything's liable to set him off.'

'God!' Steele sighed. 'There never used to be anybody on the force with feelings, now it's all touchy feely. Sure son, I'll not say a word.'

'Detective inspector Steele!' A voice behind them boomed. 'We meet again on the gruesome trail of the idiot spurned lover.'

Steele knew the voice, it sounded of a bottle of Scotch and thirty high tar cigarettes a day. Bob McLean, chief reporter for The Paisley Daily Express.

'Bobby McLean, as I live and wheeze,' Steele slapped the larger than life reporter on the shoulder. 'Why you bothering with this? Thought you would have better – maybe that's not the right choice of words – other things to write about after this morning.'

McLean sucked in what breath he could. 'Jesus what a business Rob, poor lassie. You have any ideas? Must admit it's got legs.'

Steele shook his head. 'Lots of evidence but no clues. Once we've got laughing boy here off the roof we'll get back to the station and see where we stand.'

'You'll keep me in the loop?' McLean suggested. 'Only if it's not prejudicial to the case of course.' He knew the patter.

'Not a chance Bob,' Steele smirked. 'You'd be the last person I'd tell anything to. The other papers are willing to pay cash, no questions asked, for preferential treatment.'

'Parasites,' snarled McLean. 'Just think of me as your friendly local corner shop and them as the evil conglomerate supermarkets.'

'You'll be the first to know anything Bob,' Steele reassured him. 'Those buggers will get nothing from me, not after…' he left it, and no one said a word. He had been hung out to dry by the nationals barely six months ago. Idiots printed his personal details during a drug trial at the high court! Another mistrial, he was sure the reporters were in bed with the drug barons, if they were all banged up where would they get their scoops from?

McLean lit up a cigarette, and much to Steele's chagrin, offered him one. He waved it away without saying anything. He didn't want people – some people anyway – to know that he had stopped, make that – was trying to stop. He still craved and hankered for the foul taste the tobacco left in his mouth. He hated the clean sensation, he wanted dirt. He was about to shout after McLean to tell him he had changed his mind and did, after all, want one of his high tar coffin nails when the reporter roared explosively. 'Evel K-bloody-nievel! This is magnificent! It's as though this boy's Paisley's answer to Jordan!'

'It's a cracking costume, eh?' Steele proffered.

'Amazing,' McLean cackled and coughed, his shredded wheat mop top bouncing back and forth. He pulled a digital camera from his bag. 'Anyone would think he had a diploma in media studies. He's solid gold. You couldn't make it up. At this rate he'll be pushing our dead lawyer for the front page inspector,' he laughed at Steele, the cigarette hanging limply from the side of his mouth.

'He's got every detail down to a tee.' He raised the camera to his eye and took a few quick snaps through the rising smoke of his lit cigarette.

'Can't you get somebody to do that for you?' asked Steele. 'I mean, while you're asking questions someone else could be snapping away.'

'Not a chance,' McLean snarled. 'Cutbacks. Gone are the days of scribbling in your notebook and handing it through to the typing pool then disappearing to the boozer. We're expected to do everything these days. You'll probably catch me in the newsagents one morning flogging the damn thing!' he coughed and took a close-up of the red gravel running track.

'Getting artistic now are we Bob?' Steele laughed, popping one of Mansell's mints in his mouth. He offered one to Mansell but he declined. 'Soon as this rain's off we'll get back out there and get a word with him,' he said to anyone listening. 'In the meantime,' he turned to the groundsman. 'You don't have any grub in here, do you?'

The old man pursed his lips and scowled.

'Thought not,' Steele groaned. 'I'm bloody starving.'

Five minutes later Don Black returned ladder-less, the builder's merchant had been shut right enough. Ten minutes after that they all agreed that the rain had subsided to a level that they could all cope with. Steele let McCauley and Black get back to their cycling duties. He had no intention of lifting Spencer, he'd drive him away and dump him back home if necessary, he just couldn't face the unnecessary paperwork. Not unless the boy went Tonto and started throwing stuff or assaulting people. He'd talk him down and again give him the number of a counsellor. Either that or slip him a card for a sauna, get himself sorted in a different way. Modern policing was very hands-on, he thought with a wry smile.

Steele went to shout, but had to stop himself and suppress a giggle. 'That's your fault,' he said to happy snapper Bob McLean. 'I went to call him "Frank" there.'

It was Bob McLean's turn to choke on laughter. 'Sorry,' he half chortled, half choked.

'Harry!' Steele shouted skywards. 'Do you realise that there's not a game here today?'

'That's what he said,' Spencer shouted back, pointing to the groundsman and almost losing his balance.

'Well, it's true!' Steele hollered. 'St Mirren are playing away today! At Celtic! Parkhead's the place to be at!'

The despair wiped the sparkle from Harry Spencer's eyes and his head dropped into his hands. All the while Bob McLean snapped away, and in his pocket, he hoped his Dictaphone was picking up every word.

'Why don't you come down son?' Steele asked. 'This is as much of a crowd as you're getting today.'

Spencer started berating himself, throwing his hands violently by his side and lurching to the point of dropping out of the sky. All that could be heard through the hissing of the summer rain was the word "Fuck!" repeated to the point of oblivion. He began pacing the length of the tin roof, without a thought for his footing.

'We'll have to get him down sir,' Mansell sounded genuinely worried for the sad protester. 'Either that or he's coming down quicker than he went up.'

'What do you suggest Mansell?' Steele wasn't expecting an answer.

'Don't know sir,' Mansell replied. 'It's not like we've got a trained negotiator on board.'

'Thanks for that,' Steele sighed, then cupped his hands round his mouth again and shouted, 'Harry! In the name of God, how did you get up there?'

Spencer stopped pacing for a second and pointed behind him. He muttered something, but the wind made it impossible to hear what.

'Why don't you come back down the same way then?' he shouted, before muttering, 'And my glamorous assistant Mansell here will think about giving you a shot of his wife!'

'Sir!' Mansell scowled. 'There are some things...'

Steele looked at him and shook his head, an apologetic smile forming on his lips. 'Sorry son.' He made a face as he took another sharp intake of breath. 'How the hell did he get up there? Mansell, you get round the back and see if you can find out what he's pointing to.' Mansell walked off, pulling the collar of his wet coat tighter to his chin. Steele felt every raindrop as it fell on his forehead and realised his hangover was kicking in BIGTIME- cue more nonsense rambling and forgetfulness. Up until now the alcohol had still been scurrying round his system, but not now. Now it had soured and he had miniature burrowing miners pick-axing their way through every tunnel and cavern of his alcohol-abused brain. He knew that what he needed was either to top up his booze level or sleep and never drink again. God, he needed a drink! The back of his skull felt as though it had been attacked by some poison gas, the degree of pain it caused him all encompassing. That pain was what was now foremost in his thoughts causing him not to notice Mansell shouting at him from the side of the stadium.

'Sir!' Mansell increased the volume of his hollering until he caught Steele's attention. 'Come and see this,' he waved the detective inspector towards him.

Steele and Mansell both looked to the ground and the steel-rung rope ladder that had been thrown to the ground by Spencer. All the while Bob McLean snapped away. Every time the camera clicked Steele shuddered, it sounded like he was taking a shot at him. 'He either dropped it accidentally or discarded it deliberately so we couldn't follow him up.'

'Given his past form,' Steele started, 'What would your' money be on?'

'To hell with him,' muttered Steele. 'Phone Trumpton, they can get him down with a cherry picker. I'm too hungry to be bothered with this. Come on, let's go.' He and Mansell began walking back towards the tunnel, much to the annoyance of the groundsman.

'Are you not going to arrest him?' he shouted after them.
Steele turned. 'And charge him with what? Being stupid?'

The old man mumbled as he walked with them to the tunnel and Mansell made the call to the fire brigade. As soon as he had ended the call his phone rang again. 'Sir!' he shouted after Steele. 'There's been another one.'

'Another what?' asked Steele.

'Murder,' he said coldly. 'Gallowhill.'

'Thank God for that,' Steele instantly regretted his light tone, the groundsman eavesdropping. 'For a second I thought we'd another rooftop protester on the loose.'

They got in the car without another word to the groundsman and raced their two bicycle-riding colleagues the short distance from Love street to Gallowhill.

The bike riders won, but only just. Having had the advantage of being able to cut through the back of Niddry street and straight on to the Renfrew Road whilst Mansell and Steele got caught behind every bunnetted Sunday driver on the one-way system, all oblivious to the siren. As they tore down Netherhill Road they had to avoid the drunks and junkies crossing the road at the parade of shops, before jousting with the death wish kids on their trikes and bikes on Dundonald. The car then hit every pothole on Bargarron Drive. 'Number thirteen,' Mansell said, spotting the two cyclists smirking on the pavement.

Steele stared ahead at the cyclists, his eyes boring holes in their heads. He was dismayed, after all the stops that had been pulled out up at the death on the braes carpark, this death in Gallowhill only merited "value" or "own brand" policing. All they could muster was a solitary WPC outside the close of the four in a block building. He recognised her, Constable Mhairi MacKay, first language Gaelic, transferred from some island he couldn't remember. Arse on her like a twelve-year-old boy, Steele worried about the clouds of erotic/pornographic dust that inhabited his head the day after a heavy session. He shook the image from his mind. Tonky Town they called Gallowhill, and other estates like it. Places where anything went, and it was usually your neighbour who had taken it. Like all estates, there was always a liberal sprinkling of decent hard-working souls. Steele could smell the meaty aroma of cooked breakfasts wafting the length of the street, the hard working souls were all eating fry-ups. Jammy sods! He got out of the car and walked up to the smirking

McCauley and Black. 'Don't think there's much call for Lance Armstrong and Chris Hoy here,' he snarled. 'Get back up to St Mirren Park and see that that idiot Spencer doesn't do anything dafter than he already has.'

'Shall we arrest him?' McCauley asked.

Steele sucked in some breath and shook his head. 'Warn him off, physically if you have to, the last thing we need is him turning up every other day wasting our time.'

The chastised cyclists made their way back up Bargarron Drive and turned off to the right on to the Renfrew Road.

Before entering the close Steele looked back up to the junction with Dundonald Road. Sure enough, there was Bob Mclean's battered red Mazda turning into Bargarron Drive. 'The guy in that car,' Steele pointed, instructing the WPC. 'Reporter. Watch him. I don't want him at the windows or anything. Breathalyse him if necessary.' He felt a bit bad, just a bit. McLean was a friend – of sorts – and he disliked himself for badmouthing him, but it was the job. It was always the job. He hated it, the job, made him distrust everyone, made him friendless to those not on the job. It was the only one he had ever had and it had drawn him apart from almost everyone in his life He had a constant feeling of loneliness that hung heavy on his shoulders, weighed him down, forced him deeper inside the bottle. He felt sure McLean's job had the same effect on those in his life, but, hey ho, that was his lookout. He entered the close and the stench of sour milk permeated every pore in his nostrils. 'Jesus Christ!' he pulled a hankie from his pocket and placed it over his nose.

Mansell, much younger and therefore hankie-less, held his nostrils tight together and squeaked. 'Bottom left.' He went to trace a finger on the spilt/thrown milk that covered the flaking burgundy paint of the close. It was solid. 'This must have been here months.' He shook his head. 'Used to be a nice place this you know.' They went inside. There were no carpets on the floor, just greasy dirty lino that had never been the fashion. The walls were filthy with hand prints of children. The flat smelt of the vestiges of chaotic living, take-away food and cabbage, the odour of month-old sour milk thankfully replaced. Somewhere in the flat a baby was crying.

'She's in the living room sir,' a WPC said quietly, approaching them. Beside her, Patterson looked bewildered.

'Why don't you get some air Patterson?' Steele suggested.

'I'll be fine sir,' he choked back a boak.

'Get some air. It's an order.' He made way in the narrow hallway for Patterson to pass before turning his attention to the WPC. 'Can you get on to social services about the child?'

'Children,' she corrected him. 'There's two of them, a toddler and a new born. It was the toddler that phoned.'

'Jesus, what age?' Just then a small boy, at least a week's worth of dirt on his face, entered the hall from a side bedroom. He said nothing, had no tears in his eyes, no emotion whatsoever. He merely looked up at Steele and Mansell who both fell silent at his arrival on the scene. 'What age are you pal?' Steele choked and knelt down to get eye level with the waif. He looked back at Steele with the unblinking thousand-yard stare normally associated with junkies. He didn't answer the question, just kept staring. He looked about three-and-a-half. 'Do you want to go back into your room pal, and this nice lady will have a talk to you?' He gestured for the WPC to take him back into the room.

'Then can I go and play?' he asked.

No one knew what to say as the boy ambled through to the bedroom without another word. Steele got to his feet, his head shaking. 'Poor sod. If he never stood a chance before, what hope has he got now?' Steele and Mansell edged towards the living room, first eyeing the kitchen. Food, cutlery, crockery and dirty washing all over the place.

'Do you think this was her putting up a fight or is it always like this?' Mansell wasn't really expecting an answer.

'No, it's always like this.' Steele said as a reflex. 'You'll probably find everything of value has been sold and the children have got some sort of third world illness. Fucking disgrace.'

The body of the woman was propped up facing them, sat up at a right angle just underneath the window ledge. Steele walked towards her. She appeared to have been beaten about the head, serious struggle, her hair pulled in every which direction. Her left eye was swollen, hit with something heavier than a fist. She had also been stabbed through the heart. The knife was still in her. The first thing Steele did was close the curtains and turn on the light. The lights didn't come on; the power had been turned off. He opened the end of the curtains a chink and let some light in. 'Don't want any ghouls poking their noses in,' he explained to Mansell as some sort of explanation.

'Don't know about you, sir,' Mansell started, 'but I don't think that this has anything to do with our lawyer on the braes this morning.' He sighed heavily.

'Aye,' Steele shook his head. 'This is a lover's tiff. If your two lovers happen to be thieving junkie scumbags. Probably arguing over the dregs of the last tenner bag till the Monday book gets cashed tomorrow. It's no way to live.'

'SIR!' Mansell squealed, falling backwards. 'She's breathing!'

Steele turned, and sure enough there were bubbles of bloody saliva coming from her mouth, her arms twitching involuntarily. 'Get an ambulance,' he shouted at his colleague, before running to the kitchen and coming back with a filthy towel to quell the flow of blood from her heart. As he cupped the towel round the knife the woman looked as though she was trying to say something. Steele shouted at her to keep calm, that an ambulance was on its way and she should just concentrate on breathing not talking.

As she was carried out of the close unconscious on a stretcher, head brace and oxygen mask covering her mouth Steele turned on Patterson. 'What the hell are you playing at? First rule upon entering what you suppose to be a murder scene? Check the victim's actually dead!' he shook his head, fighting the urge to knock the DS through the uneven hedge as he made his way to the steps. 'Arsehole!'

All of this was said within earshot of Bob McLean who had a Clyde-wide smile on his chops as he returned to his battered red Mazda.

6

McLean spread the Express across his desk and admired his handiwork. This had to be his best day's journalism in more years than he cared to remember. The front page banner headline SUNDAY SLAUGHTER! Filled the page. A fifty word square in the bottom right hand corner the only written detail of one of the darkest days in Paisley's recent history. Top lawyer murdered at an infamous sex spot, drug addict mother of two dying on her way to hospital after being savagely beaten in front of her children. There was a badly pixilated photograph of the car park in the sky in the left–hand corner – one day he would get the hang of the digital camera, but today it didn't matter. He had syndicated the lawyer's murder to a national red top, emphasising that there may be a sexual twist to her death. The scandal sheets loved a good sex story. They hadn't bothered to take the dead mother story from him, even though there had been a police cock-up and the girl may have lived had she been attended to sooner. Dead junkies and police cock-ups were ten-a-penny. On a lighter note, the bottom of the page banner read HAPLESS "FRANK'S" AT IT AGAIN! reference to yet another failed attempt at a rooftop protest by Harry Spencer. He allowed himself a wry smile, a stray apostrophe would change the whole mood of the front page to Sunday's Laughter. He extinguished his third cigarette of the day and decided on a shower. He pulled his robe across and rose to his feet, leaving his third black coffee of the morning untouched on the table.

He let the shower run for just under a minute to heat up, and was disrobing when he heard the door buzzer. He hadn't been expecting anyone, he'd phoned in sick to work, but surely after this coup they wouldn't be round checking up on him – not at his age. Probably some energy switch salesman, he told himself, stepping into the bath. As he stuck his head under the flow it buzzed again, this time playing out a tune. The bugger can sod off, he told himself, play all the tunes he liked. He carried on with his shower, dripping shower gel into the hair on his chest. He almost let out a yelp as he heard his front door getting clattered. A policeman's knock, he smiled. It would be that bugger Steele up to chew at his ear for the piece in the paper. Steele was the sort to break a door down rather than wait for someone to answer it, so Bob McLean shouted as loudly as he could that he wouldn't be a minute. He quickly washed the gel from his chest before switching off the shower.

He padded towards the door, towel draped round his waist and an ear to ear smile on his face. The chapping was relentless. 'Alright you old curmudgeon,' he shouted, 'I'm coming. I'm coming.' Convinced it was Steele, he didn't bother to look through his spyhole. He had made many mistakes in his life, and this would be his last.

7

Steele had spent the late afternoon and early evening drinking in Bertie's bar, he told himself it was to make sure the bar owner kept his mouth shut, but he knew he was kidding himself on. He needed drink, lots of drink, not just one. Now, in the cold light of a very painful and noisy day, he wished he hadn't. The briefing room was filling up and behind him on the boards there were more pictures than he cared to look at of Georgina McBride's lifeless body, in particular her slashed tongue. Further to the left was a solitary photograph of the murdered mother of two, Rachel Boyd. Steele sighed, having already spoken to the chief he knew exactly where the lion's share of the budget was being appropriated. They needed a result, and fast, on the McBride case. He looked on his desk at the double-page spread the lawyer's murder had been awarded in the Express, that twister McLean keen to try and establish a link between the two murders, even keener than he had been to comment upon the police incompetence at the crime scene in Gallowhill. He waited for some hush before getting to his feet, about a dozen officers in front of him.

"My name is Robert Steele and I am an alcoholic", his mischievous genes wanted to shout from the rafters, but he suppressed the urge and coughed nervously instead. 'Okay people, pin back your lugholes. Contrary to popular belief we have two murders to investigate – one easy, the other a bit more of a mystery. There will be a lot of press scrutiny, so we need to be checking and double-checking every scrap before we act on it.'

'The words pot and kettle spring to mind!' The jibe came from the back of the room, bur Steele never bothered looking up to see from whom.

'Settle down,' Steele continued, holding up a copy of The Paisley Daily Express. 'Unlike the ghouls that write for this paper,' he paused for a smile, Bob McLean – a ghoul, 'we have no reason, at this moment, to think that the two murders are in any way connected, and both cases will be investigated separately. I want two teams. Patterson, you and that poor unfortunate sitting next to you, grab a couple of uniforms and see if you can't track down this man.' The "poor unfortunate" next to him was the other John, McGlaughlin. He heard The Two Johns groan at the back of the room, but ignored it and moved across to the board and pointed to a mug shot. 'This,' he tapped the photograph, 'is Garry McCulloch. He's our killer, and as soon as the courts allow a three-year-old's evidence he'll be going down for a stretch. The boy told us it was him who "hit Mammy", but he's gone to ground somewhere, and it's your job to smoke him out. He had been living with Rachel for three months and according to the neighbours their relationship was a tad tempestuous, they thought nothing of knocking seven bells out of one another at all hours of the day. And, before you ask, yes, he is the twenty-eight-year-old junkie cousin – twice removed or some such crap – of Alisdair McCulloch, well known ne'er-do-well of the parish of Ferguslie Park. With a case like this,' he allowed himself a self-satisfied smile, 'I would start at the top and work your way down. You would have every reason to assume that Big cousin Alisdair is keen as mustard to protect his own. An upright businessman like him wouldn't want negative press coverage now, would he?'

'Ah but sir!' it was a reflex on McGlaughlin's part, but any one of the officers, having been assigned to start an investigation with Alisdair McCulloch, would have had a similar reaction. They all knew he was the main drug supplier in Paisley. They all knew he could have anyone snuffed out on a whim. They all knew that they were not in charge. They couldn't do a thing about it though, the mud they threw at him never stuck, mostly because it was deflected back at them by one of the "best" defence lawyers in the country. If you were guilty you sent for Maurice Sanderson. He was a flamboyant dresser, an eloquent speaker and one of the richest men in Scotland. He could have retired to the golf course many years previously, but his twisted mind loved the notoriety that each case he took on brought. He loved to be hated, and he loved to show how much smarter than the Crown Prosecution Service he was. He had never shirked a case yet, and had only lost two – back when he was starting out and still wet behind the ears. He vowed they would be his last, and unlike some surgeons who would shy away from potentially fatal operations, he took on everything and everyone.

Steele stared The Two Johns down and carried on. 'The rest of us will be concentrating our attentions on the McBride case, that's not to say that there won't be any overlap – if help is needed, help will be given to the Boyd case. Don't be scared to ask, you two,' he focussed on The Two Johns but they were staring at the ground like they'd found a penny and lost a major organ. 'At the moment we have to keep all avenues of enquiry open, - husband, new boyfriends – her and the husband were separated,' this news brought a cackle of enquiring "oohs" from the officers who weren't staring at the floor despairingly. Steele soon quelled their enthusiasm. 'Myself and DS Mansell have already spoken to her husband, and at the moment, we have no reason to suspect he was in any way involved. Concentrate on her work, find out who her friends were, bank details, all the usual gubbings. Myself and DS Mansell are going to her office straight after this briefing, the rest of you organise yourself. And remember, if you're not busy, assist on the Boyd case.' As they got to their feet and started muttering to each other Steele roared above them. 'Remember, absolute secrecy on this. We don't need the papers,' he scowled at the copy of The Express on the desk in front of him, 'letting out every wee detail and us being inundated with nutters wanting to salve their consciences. That means your wives and husbands, partners, dogs – button it. You know how much we all love a drop of the salacious stuff.' They were almost at the door when he remembered, 'Oh, and by the way!' he shouted. 'If you're not busy tonight around tea time you may want to tune into the local news. You may see someone you recognise,' he smirked, reference to the Chief Inspector – never off the box, they were sure he'd make an appeal for a stolen bike given half a chance. There was talk that he wore his make-up off camera as well, but no one had the bottle to get that substantiated. 'Hey,' Steele laughed, still feeling a tad drunk, 'be careful out there.'

The traffic was backed up badly on the one-way system, some idiot bus drivers thinking they could park their lumbering vehicles in the middle of the road with impunity. 'Would've been quicker bloody walking,' Steele said getting out of the car on Moss Street.

'There was nothing stopping you sir,' Mansell tried hard to disguise the annoyance in his tone. 'Might do you a bit of good to get a bit fitter, what with all your...' he was so sorry he had started that sentence, how the hell do you finish a sentence like that?

Steele finished it for him. 'Point taken son,' he closed over his door before remembering the phone he had placed in the glove compartment. He tried the handle but it was locked. Mansell hit the central locking on his key fob and the door was released. Steele leant inside and grabbed the phone. It was being held together by three elastic bands.

'A new phone wouldn't go amiss either,' added Mansell with a smirk. 'There's a shop just there,' he pointed across the road to a shop next door to the lawyers.

'Quit while you're ahead Son,' Steele smiled. They stopped outside the office and Steele moved his head in a circular motion, his neck creaking and cracking. 'Let's try and stay on the same page with this one, I'm sure the clue we're looking for is in here somewhere, so don't go shooting your mouth off at a tangent David.'

Mansell was lost for words, his mouth impersonating a feeding goldfish. It normally wasn't him who went off at tangents, and what the hell was Steele doing calling him "David"? Was he getting soft? What was he doing showing him any respect whatsoever? Was he setting Mansell up for a fall? Was Mansell's over-elaborate imagination firing off at a tangent? 'Fair enough sir,' Mansell coughed nervously. 'I'll try to follow your lead.'

The ground floor reception echoed with the tinny sound of the bell attached to the door. Steele and Mansell looked around at the sparse surroundings, an empty desk, no computer, a small sofa pinned to the wall where clients were kept waiting, cheap wood flooring, no pictures or paintings on the walls and a bland panelled door that obviously led upstairs. 'Hardly burst a gut on the décor,' Steele smiled. 'You'd have thought that with it being a group of women lawyers there would have been flowers and pot-pourri coming out of every available orifice…' he was stopped in his tracks by someone coming through the panelled door.

'Can I help you?' A middle-aged woman looked down her nose at them. A good trick as she stood nearly a foot below the two of them. Steele felt there was something of the Jean Brodie about her, everything proper, everything in its place. He doubted she had a smouldering secret though, she looked as though "all that" was behind her now.

Mansell was the first to pull out his warrant card. 'It's about Ms McBride,' he said, his voice rueful and calm. 'This is DI Steele and I'm DS Mansell.'

The woman eyed Mansell's card and turned her attention to Steele who had yet to produce his ID. Reluctantly he did so, her gaze too stern for the time of the morning. 'Quite right to be suspicious,' he informed her. 'Now if you don't mind we'd like access to Georgina's files, miss…' He waited for the woman to state her name, but she seemed to have no intention of doing so, the fact that her lip curled when Steele said the word "Georgina" testament to her having taken an instant dislike to the detective inspector for the familiar way he spoke about her boss.

'Can we have your name please Madam?' Mansell butted in, knowing that at any moment Steele was going to tear her head off.

'Is it important who I am?' her composure seemed to be swithering somewhat, her once-terse lip now trembling slightly. 'What's important is that you catch the monster who did this to Ms McBride.'

Steele grunted audibly.

'Exactly Madam,' agreed Mansell, throwing a look at Steele. 'that's why it's important that we get as much information as possible on Ms McBride, her client list, her colleagues, friends, enemies...'

'She had no enemies!' The woman blurted out.

'She obviously had at least one,' Steele couldn't help himself. 'Now, Ms...'

'It's Mrs,' she corrected him, her composure restored. 'Mrs Gregg. Isla.'

'And what do you do here Isla?' Steele didn't mean to, but he knew how patronising he sounded.

'Reception,' she replied.

'Excellent,' Steele sounded a tad more convincing now. 'How long?'

'Since it opened,' Isla Gregg's eyes glazed over. 'Since the beginning,' she choked back a tear.

Mansell made to place a comforting hand on her shoulder, but Steele saw the movement of his hand and stopped him. With her head bowed Isla Gregg had seen nothing. Steele carried on, 'You're probably the very person we need to be talking with,' He paused long enough to allow her a quizzical look at him. 'Everyone knows that there is nothing happens in any office or workplace that the receptionist doesn't know about, and I'm not talking gossip or tittle-tattle here,' Steele added by way of reassurance. 'I bet you could tell me what case almost everyone in the office upstairs was working on right at this minute if you had to?'

Isla paused for a second, the cogs in her head starting again. 'I suppose I could,' she answered, somewhat surprised at herself.

'And yet you don't even know it,' Steele smiled, 'don't know what an important part you play in the whole scheme of things in this law office?'

The tears that seemed to be coming had been suppressed and a glimmer of a smile appeared for the first time on the receptionist's face. Steele looked at Mansell, whose nose seemed convinced it could smell bullshit.

'As you no doubt know,' Steele continued, 'the first twenty-four hours after a crime are vital. As we had no access to the offices yesterday, these will count as the first twenty-four as far as we're concerned. We would like access to all the files, particularly those Ms McBride was dealing with personally. Do you think that will be a problem?' he asked charmingly. 'We'll also need to talk to all the staff individually. It would probably be better done here than at the station, so I was wondering if you could also set us up in an office?'

'I don't think it will be a problem,' she bit on her bottom lip. 'You could use Georgina's.'

She took them upstairs to the main office where they were greeted by a sea of inactivity. All the staff standing round the expensive looking coffee machine. Steele addressed them, told them not to disappear, that they would all have to be interviewed. Isla Gregg then showed them to Georgina McBride's office at the far end of the room. The office was sparse, no filing cabinet, a large desk with a laptop to one side of it. Steele sat down on what was obviously Georgina's chair behind the desk. Plush leather with padded armrests. Mansell grabbed the other chair, also leather, but less padding on it, and wheeled it round to join him the other side of the desk. They interviewed the staff and gained nothing, she was loved and respected by them all, no sign of the usual office bitchiness that Steele knew existed in most workplaces inhabited by more than one woman. As the last of the women left the office they knew they had drawn a blank, they knew nothing of her private life, indeed her marriage break-up was news to them all.

'There you are gents!' Jane, a paralegal instructed by the receptionist to assist the "two gentlemen" was back with a folder containing a printout of the cases the company had taken on in the past three months. 'If any of these catch your eye give me a shout and I'll pull up the file on computer.' She smiled warmly at Mansell, who had moved to the other side of the desk from Steele. 'I'll get you some more coffee. How do you take it?'

'Just milk thanks,' Mansell replied. 'If it's not too much trouble.'

She was walking away as Steele shouted after her. 'Just milk with mine as well, thanks.'

She turned and looked back at him, not really apologising. 'Okay,' before looking at Mansell again as though she was telling him she understood his pain.

Steele laughed playfully across the table at him. 'I'll tell your wife.'

'Sir,' Mansell was flustered. 'I can assure you, I didn't, I don't...'

'Can't help being a stud, eh?' Steele suggested. 'I had the same trouble myself once. Just the once, mind.' He opened the buff file and pulled out the loose sheets of A4. He took half for himself and passed the rest over to his embarrassed colleague.

'What are we looking for sir?'

'Needle, haystack, you get the idea?' Steele replied, starting to read the case names in front of him. 'Is that too technical for you son?'

'Think I'll muddle through sir, thanks for your concern though.' Mansell placed the papers on the desk and began scanning.

They sat and read in silence, occasionally one of them smiling or frowning at the nuances of the details they were taking in. About an hour after they started Mansell felt he had found something. 'Sir,' he whispered, pushing a document across the desk. 'Take a look at this.'

'Well, well, and indeed, well,' Steele exhaled and scanned the rest of the paper. 'Now that is interesting. Jean McCulloch petitioning for divorce against her husband Alisdair. Physical and mental cruelty. Is there a date on this thing?'

'It's ehm..., it was ongoing sir,' Mansell replied. 'The case opened back in May.'

'I can't imagine Alisdair McCulloch being too pleased at some hotshot lawyer poking about in his finances trying to get an unfair share for his wife.'

'No doubt Sanderson would've been all over it,' said Mansell.

'Jesus!' scowled Steele. 'Get your new girlfriend to pull up the details on this,' he instructed Mansell. 'I'll phone that tit McGlaughlin, hopefully the lazy bastard's not started yet or this case is pumped before we've even blown any air into it.'

McGlaughlin answered after six rings, obviously trying to concoct a plausible excuse for Steele as to why he hadn't started interviewing Alisdair McCulloch yet.

'McGlaughlin!' Steele barked before he had a chance to say anything.

'Sir,' McGlaughlin gulped.

'Tell me you're nowhere near our man McCulloch yet.'

'We're just getting on to it sir,' he lied.

'Don't,' he growled. 'Don't do anything. In fact, don't even leave the station. There's been a development and I'll be dealing with it personally.'

'Sir?'

'It's not for you to worry about,' he told him dismissively. 'You and the other John can go away out and book some speeding cars or something,' Steele clicked the phone off. Steele knew that most other detectives would have been straight on the phone to his superiors being shut out of such an important case like that, but not McGlaughlin, he was plodding along until his pension matured, doing as little as possible in the meantime. Conviction quotas and arrest rates were a foreign language to him, very much a background figure in the force.

'We need to get this lot back to Mill street,' Steele said to Mansell as he came back with an armful of folders. 'I'll get the Two Johns to read through it. I think even they are capable of underlining with felt tips.' He smirked. 'Come on,' Steele rose to his feet.

'Be right there sir,' Mansell answered. 'Need to use the facilities.' He indicated to the toilet.

'Remember and put the seat back down or this lot will lynch you,' Steele smiled. 'See you outside.' He took the folder from Mansell and headed for the stairs. He needed some air, his hangover biting.

As he opened the door and stepped into the rain he was sure his tongue was sweating and had to swallow hard to stop himself from gagging. Drookit figures floundered on their not so merry way past The Last Post and into the refuge of The Piazza. He felt sure he recognised the back of one of the people entering the shopping centre. It was hard to tell, but it certainly looked like the rat's tail anti-hairdo of Garry McCulloch, suspect numero uno. The more he stared, the less he saw, the rain battering on his face, droplets clinging to his eyelashes and clouding his vision. All junkies looked the same to him anyway – like Jesus if they were male or Mary Magdelene if female. He fumbled for his phone, trying not to drop the folder, but by the time he located it Mansell was at his back.

'Thought you'd be at the car by now.'

'I think I've just spotted McCulloch's cousin going into The Piazza.' Steele told him. 'Phone Control, get some uniforms out the pie shops and into there.'

The two men made their way smartly to the front entrance of the shopping centre, Mansell with the phone glued to his ear, the battering rain making it difficult to hear. By the time he finished his call they were inside, approaching The Post Office. They looked inside, and it was Mansell who spotted the group loitering inside. Four junkies, one female, three male. The female and one other stood over McCulloch who was crouching with another man, as though posing for a football photograph, talking conspiratorially about everything and nothing at all. As soon as McCulloch saw the two men in suits enter he dropped his head to face the ground, hoping they hadn't seen him.

'You looking for inspiration McCulloch?' Steele asked as they approached. 'Cause it's a bit late in the day for you to be learning to tie your shoe laces.' The junkie's trainers were like those of almost everyone else under thirty, untied with the laces poked inside. Steele hated it, what had obviously started out as fashion statement by some idiot boy years ago was now a testament to the backward nature of society in general – if they didn't need to use it, why learn it?

'What is it?' McCulloch answered, adenoidal whine to the fore. Where the hell did they learn to talk like that as well? Steele was a man out of time, trapped by his desire to give almost everyone a good shake and get them to buck up their ideas.

'You know fine well what it is?' sighed Steele. 'The name Rachel Boyd ring any bells with you, maybe one of the seven bells you knocked out of her yesterday?'

The mention of her name caused audible adenoidal intakes of breath from the other junkies. 'Don't know what you're talking about.' McCulloch got to his feet, he was eye-level with Steele. 'Do you know who I am?'

'Why have you forgotten?' Mansell chipped in bursting to laugh. He loved it when the wideos of Paisley threw him a ball like that. He just kept his eye on it and batted it clean out the park.

'What?' McCulloch seemed genuinely upset that the two men hadn't melted to a mere puddle of water when he said his last remark. His cousin Aldo was one of the most feared men in Paisley. He felt he was owed some deflected respect.

'Of course we know who you are,' started Steele. 'Garry McCulloch, I'm arresting you for the murder of...' As he went to grab hold of McCulloch's wrist Mary Magdelene grabbed his hand and sunk her teeth into the flesh between his thumb and index finger.

Steele's reflexes kicked in and he pulled his right hand away before his left fist came up and punched the girl and she fell into a display espousing the virtues of taking out travel insurance when venturing abroad. The scream that came from her throat was decidedly feral catching everyone in The Post Office off guard. Everyone stared in the direction it came from. It was Monday morning, there were more people in the erstwhile giro/pension shop than went to most St Mirren home games. About one hundred and fifty pairs of eyes watched as the girl leapt like a banshee and clung to Steele's right shoulder, teeth-bared. Steele turned sharply to try and remove her, noting that McCulloch was on the lamb, heading deeper into the engrossed crowd waiting in their various lines. He was going straight into them, deeper into a dead end, thought Steele as he pushed his attacker's head to the side, where Mansell grabbed her shaking shoulders and wrestled her to the ground, careful of the biting teeth, flailing punches and kicking feet. Dervishes had nothing on her, cartoon Tasmanian devils would have run and hid.

As Steele passed his cuffs to Mansell he saw that the rest of the junkies had bolted, leaving a lassie to fight their battles. Albeit, a fairly able lassie. Mansell wrestled The Dervish round so that her face was munching carpet. 'Where's McCulloch?' he looked up at Steele. He was busy squeezing at his bleeding hand, trying to force the girl's saliva from him before it had the chance to infect anything.

'He went that-a-way!' he pointed to the counter, knowing it to be a dead end, but stared in dismay as McCulloch, his path cleared by terrified pensioners bounded onto the counter and vaulted the Perspex that protected the post office workers from the baying public. The baying public gasped as he landed on the other side, pushing staff out of the way before eventually disappearing through a door that led to the fire exit that came out on Central Way. 'Bollocks!' Steele knew they had lost him, the back door was always open, the staff more concerned about getting their nicotine fix than any robber sneaking in and robbing The Post Office of everything. It was a blag waiting to happen, all thanks to the smoking ban.

He tried to grab his phone from his right pocket with his left hand, but he found it difficult, his trousers were sticking to his legs from the deluge of rain. He had no need to anyway, for a second later three uniformed officers were by his side. He despatched them to Central Way and told them to contact control. He watched in chagrin as all three of them went right towards an exit, not one of them smart enough to take the exit to the left. McCulloch would evade them, of that he was now certain, what with Mack Sennnet directing the police force! He looked out the window and saw more uniforms swarming towards the Post Office, he pointed left and two of them followed his directions, sprinting to the exit by the sandwich shop that led out to Smithhill Street.

The other Uniforms entered the Post Office expecting a riot, but were met with only one cuffed prisoner, a female at that. 'Watch her,' Mansell instructed as he tried to get her to her feet. 'She's a biter!' Mary Magdelene tried to wrestle herself free, but three burly officers smothered her every attempted move. They led her out into The Piazza away from the noise that now engulfed the Post Office. Chatter about who had done what and who had hit whom and how high did he jump and on and on and on. The stories getting bigger and gathering more details with the speaking of every word. Any minute now McCulloch would have acquired a knife, then a gun, then a tank. Embellishment was necessary if the people of Paisley weren't to drown in their own miserable tears. For if this was all there was... This, waiting in a queue to cash your giro or pension, would surely force the whole population into a brick–filled bag to be tossed into The White Cart at the earliest convenience. People needed more, they needed embellishment in their lives, and with the shutting of yet another shop/pub, the people of Paisley needed embellishment more than most.

'The hospital I think for you sir,' suggested Mansell.'

'Tout suite young man,' Steele replied. 'Tout suite.'

Mansell scrunched up his eyes at the outpouring of nonsense that came from his boss's mouth. 'Think you've got blood poisoning sir.'

'Aye,' sighed Steele, 'that's the best prognosis I can hope for.'

8

With his free right hand, he turned the dial of the shower to the right, turning the water temperature down by a couple of degrees. His left had a hold of his soapy penis, he was coaxing it out of its shell. It didn't take much persuading, all he had to do was to shut his eyes and imagine the look of surprise on McLean's face. He tried hard not to think too much about the details of the face though, blotchy from bad food, boozer's nose - a poppy about to blossom into life. He imagined McLean's face unconscious from the blow, the way the knife scratched at the bones of his fingers. Not so much blood as with the tart, no gushing torrents. He felt himself stiffen fully now and looked down delightedly at his angry cock in his left hand. He hadn't been like this with Charlotte in ages, hardly at all since the twins. For five years almost, and this thing between his legs – this magnificent specimen – had been hibernating, slumbering as though dead. And now this, since that Sunday he had been almost permanently engorged. An unexpected bonus to his extracurricular activities. His expression was halfway between a snarl and a smile. Extracurricular activities? If Charlotte were here now, well... If she hadn't taken his boys and gone to her mother's to "get her head straight". What the hell was that all about? What more did she fucking need? A good house in a good area? A good job, the boys lined up for a half decent primary school? She was a... he looked down at his cock, no longer angry, but weather-beaten. Actually, if Charlotte was here now she'd be telling him to "put it away" whilst she got on with some unnecessary hoovering, dusting or some other pointless cleaning. He often wondered if she was seeing someone else, getting savagely banged while he worked at the coal-face to bring home the veggie bacon substitute. She used to like it. Jesus, she used to love it when she was pregnant, at him every morning before he left for work. He'd get there paranoid that he stank of it, reeked of spunk like a spotty schoolboy discovering the joys. He grabbed himself tighter, he was stiff again, imagining what it would be like to put it in the place she would never let him. He tried a few times when she was drunk, but to her it was always an exit! He closed his eyes, saw Georgina McBride's mouth gushing with blood, before opening them again, just in time to see his thin hot sperm arc and fall into the ravine of water heading for the plughole.

9

Bain's face was more beetroot than usual, unfathomable rage steaming from his cauliflower ears. Ears that had grown larger with the passing of the years, moulded originally on the rugby fields of the Borders. 'How the hell could you let him get away like that? You had him in your grasp man.'

Steele was scunnered, held up his bandaged hand and felt like showing the chief super the recent tetanus jab in his backside but thought better of it. Collective responsibility always felt personal when doled out to him and him alone by Bain. 'The curse of every postman sir,' Steele smiled. 'Bitten by a dog in the course of my duties.'

'Ach I don't know what this town's coming to,' Bain shook his head. 'It's ever since those liberal lefties banned the tawse. Bloody kids have no idea what discipline is. What's happening with the girl?'

'A.B.H,' replied Steele. 'But she's not saying a word until her legal eagle turns up. You know what they're like, don't fart unless they've got a brief in close proximity.'

A smile at last crackled across Bain's Halloween cake of a face. 'Who's the lawyer?'

Steele examined his loafers, sensing his whole life was heading downwards. 'Sanderson.'

Bain seemed visibly taken aback. 'That bugger!' he scowled. They moved in the same circles, belonged to the same clubs and associations, but that seemed only to turn Bain further against him. 'He's the biggest scoundrel in Christendom! Got to be something fishy going on, I mean she's a...'

'Drug-addled prostitute sir,' interrupted Steele. 'Whose bite is as bad as her bark.'

'It would seem so.' Bain scratched at the lobe on his hairy left ear. 'McCulloch's obviously behind it, covering every inch of his back now that Jeanie's finally caught him with his pants down!' he was almost laughing.

The fine line, the one between right and wrong, good and evil, was almost invisible sometimes, Steele mused. Here was the Chief Inspector talking about one of the most evil drug baron's in Paisley as though he was an old school chum. The death, misery and chaos that this man caused just for the sake of making more money than his febrile imagination could deal with. The line disappeared with money, when some thought about money, it was just about having it, didn't matter a fuck where it came from. 'Aye sir.' Steele sighed. 'Mansell's scouring through her record now, making sure we know where we stand when Sanderson traps.'

'Good, good,' Bain cleared his throat. 'David's the sort of chap who won't be standing still, smart as a whip, going places. What about this damnable shoe pervert that's reared his ugly head again? We any further forward on nabbing him?'

Steele huffed. 'Manpower problem sir, the weekend's events have us chasing our tails. If we could free up some overtime money from the budgets, then maybe we could think about it.'

It was Bain's turn to huff, his face contorting. 'Can't see that being possible Robert.'

Steele knew the mere mention of overtime would be enough to shut Bain up about the "shoe pervert". Catching him ranked alongside nailing Harry Spencer for sheer stupidity. He was a bee in Bain's bonnet though, one of his niece's had been his third "victim". So far there were five "victims", all approached outside school gates by a nondescript balding man in his fifties. Who distracted them with some pointless conversation before grabbing one of their shoes and running off. All different types of shoes and trainers, didn't seem to matter to him. It was posted in the "weird" filing cabinet.

'Anyway Robert,' Bain patted his shoulder. 'I'm off to crunch some numbers. Keep me abreast of any developments.' He headed down the corridor towards his office.

Steele paused, watching the big man get smaller with every step. The force had changed since he had first started. It used to be that they were all in it together, them against the plebs, but now everyone was watching their own backs and sticking their knives into everyone else's. Steele keyed the number in the door and walked down the corridor towards his own office. When he got there Mansell was seated behind his desk, clicking frantically at the laptop.

'Hope you don't mind sir?' he half asked.

'Knock yourself bandy son,' replied Steele. 'Our glorious leader has just been singing your praises on the stairwell.'

'Chief Inspector Bain?' Mansell almost gulped, feeling himself getting slightly embarrassed.

'The very same,' Steele responded, sitting on a chair the other side of the desk. 'Says you're a lad that's going places.'

'Really?' Mansell tried hard to be nonchalant.

'Yeah,' Steele fished in his pocket and pulled out a tenner. 'He suggested the canteen for a roll with square sausage and a bacon and tattie scone doubler.' He pushed the note towards his assistant.

'Very good,' Mansell reached across and took the note, then got to his feet. 'Anything else?'

'Make sure it's as greasy as possible,' Steele added. 'Then we can face that slimeball Sanderson on an even footing. Get yourself something. Coffee as well.'

'Of course sir,' Mansell turned the handle on the door. 'You don't mind if I opt for a healthy option, do you?' He didn't wait for an answer.

'When did this turn up?' Steele picked up a padded buff envelope from the desk.

'Don't know,' Mansell had pulled the door open. 'Was there when I came in.' With that he set off on his errand.

Steele picked it up and sniffed it, even though it had obviously been scanned. Nothing, not even a rogue Scotch pie got into the Mill Street without being checked for alien bodies. It read, ROB STEAL, MILL STREET POLICE STATION, PAISLEY. The address looked as though it had been written by a child, Steele's name more of an instruction than a moniker. He shook the envelope, more out of instinct than anything else, the bubble wrap interior masking the contents from giving away any tell-tale noise. There was nothing else for it. He opened the envelope. He looked inside and pulled out a DVD, no casing, just the disc, and a scrap of paper, again written in childish scrawl. THE RENFREWSHIRE ROPE AND TWINE COMPANY!!! That was it, no kisses, "ps's" or "love you's". Worse still, no name. He held the disc up and it twinkled brightly, deflecting the light from the overhead strip lighting. The refraction made him think of "The Dark Side of the Moon", an album he'd had since he was a spotty teenager. Still had it somewhere. With the passing of time and technology his vinyl albums had travelled further up the house. From living room, to spare bedroom. From spare bedroom to loft. They'd be staging a rooftop concert next.

He looked at the screen of the laptop. Mansell was doing something, defragmenting or some other nonsense, he hated the way computer language alienated him. Pieces of the screen were tumbling down in brightly coloured chunks. He thought about pressing the escape button repeatedly, his default setting when confronted with an unruly computer, but decided against it. He'd wait for Mansell and his breakfast to arrive before tackling anything as technical as playing a DVD.

Five minutes and two stomach rumbles later Mansell arrived with the fodder. Before he sat down Steele asked him, 'Renfrewshire Rope and Twine Company?' he gratefully received the brown paper bag. 'Ring any bells?'

Mansell's brow creased. 'Nope, should it?'

'This,' Steele handed over the DVD and scrap of paper, 'was inside the envelope.'

'What's on it?' Mansell held up the disc.

Steele shrugged, 'Dunno, I've been waiting on you to stop doing whatever it is you're doing on this computer.'

'Oh right,' Mansell took a bite of his tuna roll and leant over and pulled the laptop towards him. His fingers danced like a pianists across the keyboard and the DVD player slowly opened. He gingerly placed the disc in, the granary roll now balanced precariously between his teeth.

His fingers danced for a second time and the two men sat waiting for the show to begin.

Mansell's roll dropped from his mouth to the desk at the same time as Steele's potato scone fell helplessly to the floor.

'Bloody hell!' Muttered Mansell.

Steele was aghast, 'What the f...'

10

He had too much time on his hands, too many hours waiting, waiting for the next one, the next victim. He wondered how his counterpart in rival operations filled these dead hours. He had seen them read papers (the broadsheets sometimes!) from cover to cover. He had seen them reading books, nipping into bookies, into cafes. He could do all that, although the broadsheets interested him not a jot. The books neither, every work of fiction he had attempted to read since leaving school had been an unfinished symphony. Stig of the Dump had been the last book he had picked up with any purpose, except his "Bible", but that was a mandatory requirement of his profession. Of course, it was all online now. He had seen them fill their time with that – laptops connected to the internet. That was a no no as well, cyberspace was not so much a grey area for him as a black hole. He had no need of a computer, he had his notebooks that he kept all his dates in, all the information he needed contained within them. All the things he still had to do with his victims, all their flaws that they would pay through the nose for. He spent most of his "live" time exploiting the flaws, picking at the sores of his victims until they either healed totally or left a vast gaping wound.

There were others in his shoes, others he hated, but secretly admired. The shaggers. They found it easy, either with their victims, or with former victims to hump their way through the quiet times. Lonely women with even more free time on their hands than them. He had thought this to be a myth (the permissive society), maybe because it never happened to him, but he had seen them. Had seen them parked outside houses that weren't their own, their cars empty and the curtains closed. He couldn't do that. Had never done that. Had never even been offered the chance, wouldn't know what to do now if he was. His cock had taken unofficial strike action since he had started losing his hair. Now, five years into being follically challenged he knew all the bullshit about bald men being more virile to be just that, a steaming pile...

He might not have been sexually active the way the shaggers were, but he had his own thing. The thing he shared with no one. If he was honest, this was how he filled in his spare time, but it was getting more and more difficult. There were people everywhere! Gone were the days when he could pull up in a quiet street and simply pull one out the boot and indulge himself in the driver's seat. There was always someone looking, if not in person, then from on high. Cameras everywhere. A couple of years ago he had become obsessed with spotting them, but with the driving down of every road and the passing of time he knew there was nowhere. Nowhere in this town he could openly partake of his thing, his wee obsession. Not even in the pervert's clubs.

He had tried them, well, tried one and it had been a disaster. Tried and failed, like a pre-pubescent teenager in a changing room full of hairy rugby players passing round a hooker. He thought that going there would ignite the long dormant flame in his libido, he had seen things like it on the TV (in Germany mostly) and had been surprised when he found out that the same sort of establishment could be found in any major town or city, even Paisley!

It was all a matter of knowing where to look, and his profession had enabled him the luxury of looking round every street and every building in the town. He had first spotted the strange goings on one Saturday evening a few months previously. An uneventful lesson from Gallowhill via Broomlands Street en route to the Linwood dual carriageway had been enlivened considerably as he passed the crematorium and noticed some seriously smart parked cars just beyond the gates. Beamers, Mercs, Audis. The west end was famed for one thing, effluence rather than affluence. On his left, built into the tenements was a strange looking shop front – no windows, just a facade of what appeared to be rotting timber and a bleak sign proclaiming that inside this gloomy exterior was something called The Renfrewshire Rope and Twine Co. He saw someone going into it, someone he recognised, and whom he knew had nothing to do with the ancient art of rope making. He was more of a story teller, the lawyer that was never off the TV, Maurice Sanderson.

The lesson carried on with its' usual banality, his victim was ready for her test, of that he was sure, but he would pick at a few more scars, open up some old wounds and make her doubt her ability and book a few more lessons. Her next couple of lessons would concentrate on reversing around a corner, that would shake her. He was sure he could get at least another hundred quid out of her no bother. On the way back he instructed her to turn left into Broomlands Street and this time upon passing the supposedly closed shop he saw a blond stunner exit a shiny black Audi and confidently ring the doorbell. She wore heels the size of scaffolds and her skirt as a belt. He never saw much more, but when he looked in the rear view mirror she was gone, gobbled up by The Renfrewshire Rope and Twine Co.

Over the course of the next few weeks he made a point of daily passing the boarded up shop. He saw more activity and wondered, wondered if it was the sort of place he could display his obsession in public. He felt sure they would, if the lengths of the skirts and dresses were anything to go by.

He simply turned up one Saturday, told Belinda he had lessons until nine and she had swallowed it. He parked the car (the tell-tale learner plates and rooftop display removed and placed in the boot) and walked as confidently as he could towards the closed door, conscientiously ignoring the camera he saw out the corner of his eye. He rang the doorbell, his palms sweating and his mouth dry. Just as the door was opening a car pulled up behind him. He instinctively looked – the shiny black Audi again. He turned his attention back to the dickie-bowed doorman who said nothing, merely looked at him questioningly.

'I'd like in,' he tried to say as casually as possible.

The doorman didn't reply.

'How much is it?' he was getting that sinking feeling – "Yer name's not down, ye're not getting in" feeling.

He began fumbling with his wallet, pulling out a card. It was his points card for the filling station at the supermarket!

'Stop teasing him Davie!' he heard the voice behind him, as seductive as a freshly opened box of chocolates. He then felt a hand on his bald pate. 'It might be a bit of fun, you know what they say about bald men?'

He turned and saw the blond bombshell from weeks before, the plunging neckline of her dress drawing his eyes immediately to her magnificent alabaster breasts. She had an aura of Chanel No 5 about her that almost made him cry.

'No problem Miss McBride,' Davie replied with a wink, standing to the side. 'You folks enjoy yourself now.'

The woman walked down the dark hallway with him in silence as he spluttered his gratitude like the pre-pubescent in the changing room being presented with a warm soft hand on his flaccid member. The woman in the sparkly dress guided him upstairs and when they got to the top of the stairs and another door she spoke confidently. 'What's your name?'

'Blair,' he held out his hand but she refused it with a knowing smile.

'Blair,' she rang the bell. 'This isn't the kind of place you can pay in to. It's invitation only. Remember that tonight and act accordingly. Don't charge off like a dog with two dicks.'

The door was opened and Blair looked inside. He couldn't believe what he was seeing.

11

'I don't believe what I'm seeing,' Steele loosened his tie and pointed at the screen of the laptop. 'This, this is happening in Paisley?'

'It would appear so,' Mansell had stopped looking at the action and was concentrating on the background. 'It's over a month since this was made.' He pointed to the date on the left-hand bottom corner of the screen, away from the people bang at it on the film, naked save for some cardboard celebrity masks. Right now the action centred on Piers Morgan being straddled by Lady Gaga.

'Seventh of May?' Steele nodded.

Mansell shook his head. 'It's American,' he said to the senior officer. 'The month's always at the start, it's the Fifth of July. It's over a month old.'

'Even so,' Steele was aghast. 'I still can't believe that this is happening in Paisley. Let's get over there. Find out where this Renfrewshire Rope and Twine Co. is. If nothing else, we'll get a good laugh.'

'I looked online,' Mansell replied. 'Nothing.'

Steele fished in his drawer and threw a book at him - The Yellow Pages. 'Let's do it the old fashioned way.'

Mansell looked under "rope", "twine", "Renfrewshire", "cable", "thread" and finally "string" before eventually giving up. 'Doesn't exist,' he put the book down on the desk. 'Not in there anyway,' he nodded at the formerly glorious yellow directory on the desk. 'I'll try online again on a different search engine.'

'You do that,' Steele rose to his feet. 'I'll get us a coffee.'

'Tea for me,' Mansell didn't even look up from his screen.

Steele scowled, 'I knew that.' He just knew that "I'll get myself a coffee – black, one sugar and you a tea with just milk" was too much of a mouthful, and "I'll get us a beverage" made him sound like too much of a twat.

When he came back from the canteen Mansell was still looking blankly at the monitor. 'Nothing, no mention of it anywhere, must be really secretive.'

'Bollocks!' Steele placed the drinks on the desk. 'Was talking to McCauley, our resident Bradley Wiggins, and he told me it's a disused workshop on Broomlands Street, next to that Indian that does the good spinach dish your wife's always raving about.'

A light bulb clicked resplendent atop Mansell's head. 'So it is, knew it rang a bell.'

'Aye right,' Steele pushed his tea across the desk to him. 'We'll have our beverage first.' He felt like laughing but didn't.

'Beverage, eh?' Mansell smiled as he tentatively picked up his tea – it was always scalding when Steele went for it.

'It's a long story,' Steele sighed and sucked at his coffee.

Twenty-five minutes later Mansell parked the car directly outside The Renfrewshire Rope and Twine Co. and wondered if he had the right place. 'You sure about this?' he asked Steele. Like the closed down dance school next door to it, The Renfrewshire Rope and Twine Co. was built into the bottom floor of a row of sandstone tenements that had long since had their day. The facade of The Renfrewshire Rope and Twine Co. appeared to be just that, a decidedly unimposing frontage that detailed nothing and concealed everything of what went on inside if the DVD they had received was in any way accurate. It was an all wooden front, hazelnut brown panels hidden under a hundred years of dust that had gathered on it - Mr Sheen would have had to call for reinforcements. The font of the letters was like nothing Mansell had seen on any computer screen, perhaps done before the advent of the microchip by a now long dead sign writer. The two men exited the car and rounded a puddle before approaching the front door of the business.

'This is a wild goose chase,' Steele ran the index finger of his right hand down one of the wooden panels. 'I mean,' he held up a dust-coated digit. 'That's a disgrace. If this is some kind of knocking shop then it's clearly for the downmarket, downtrodden, tracksuit-wearing members of the community, not lawyers and the like.'

'Mmm,' Mansell pressed a button on the intercom system to the side of the indistinct wood panelled door and was clearly none too flabbergasted when he heard no sound coming from inside. No buzz, no bell, no heavy footsteps dashing to the door. Not even an echo. He rolled his eyes to the raining sky.

'You'll not get anybody in there the noo!' A voice above him shouted.

He and Steele focussed on the voice. Thirty foot above them a woman's face peered out a top floor window, bingo winged arms and a jowly pig's face that had seen at least sixty-five years on the planet. 'There's nobody there son, the freaks only come out on a Saturday night. You'll not catch them in just noo.'

'Will we not, the noo?' Steele mocked. 'Who's your landlord dear?' he asked.

She shouted down a reply and Steele instructed Mansell back to the car. As they were doing so there was more shouting from above. 'Can you just nip to the shop for me, just for fags?'

'Sure,' Steele smirked. 'I'll do that and you can sit at that window and watch me. How does that sound?'

'I'll write it doon.' She disappeared into the flat.

Mansell looked at Steele, he didn't mind driving him here and there, but going messages for a flabby old crone, no way.

Steele threw him a frown. 'Get in the car,' he laughed.

As Mansell indicated to pull out the two men saw some coins wrapped in scrunched up paper land on the bonnet of the car. Mansell was too exasperated to notice that they didn't bounce off, but simply nestled into the dent they had created in his car. He checked his mirror and drove off.

'Scrambles aren't what they used to be, are they?' Steele smirked.

12

Maurice Sanderson's law firm occupied a fading sandstone Victorian building a stones throw from the court building. Like many a structure in the town it had formerly been a textile workplace – a carpet factory, and iconic monochrome photographs of looms and focussed workers were hung at strategic points in the reception hall to remind those who worked and visited there of its history. That's what Sanderson told the council anyway, before they handed over their grant to him for keeping a semblance of the building's history intact. The few tourists who trawled through the reception hall in the summer a small price to pay for the annual cash bonanza. Sanderson had always believed that money came to money, and he had no desire to disprove the theory. Steele entered through the swing doors, a sneer starting to form as he approached the dolly bird receptionist. The place was a far cry from Georgina McBride's office – all show. He asked to see Sanderson and was told he was busy in a meeting. He showed his warrant card and the receptionist felt differently about Sanderson's availability. She made a call and Maurice Sanderson came down in the lift to meet them – all of two flights of stairs.

'D.I. Steele!' he boomed and held out his hand which Steele refused. 'How can I be of assistance?' His confidence seemed to instantly drain as his hand hung limply in mid-air.

'You could start by telling me about The Renfrewshire Rope and Twine Company and the goings on therein at the weekends.' Steele smiled as the smugness dripped from the lawyer's face and on to the floor. 'How's that for an opening gambit? You're in the movies!'

'Excellent,' Maurice Sanderson straightened his tie and unbuttoned the jacket of his Saville Row pinstripe. 'Perhaps it would be best if we spoke in my office.' He motioned to put his hand to the detective's back, but the withering look Steele presented him with persuaded him to do otherwise. 'No calls Samantha. None whatsoever.'

The two men were silent in the lift, even though they were the only ones in it. The silence was broken by Steele as soon as the door to Sanderson's office was shut behind him. 'So, Maurice spill the beans.' He said matter of fact. 'We've seen you in a video,' he paused and corrected himself, 'dvd, film, call it what you will. Don't think the costume department will win any Oscars, considering not one bugger in it was wearing a stitch. As I recall all you were wearing was a mask. Always thought you should be wearing one.' He had sat down in Sanderson's chair and the lawyer stood beside him waiting for him to move. He would have a wait, and eventually Maurice Sanderson sat in the chair he reserved for his clients, shuffling into it uncomfortably.

He was unabashed. 'I've seen the same film.' He crossed his legs. 'Have you any clues who made it, what they're up to? Is it blackmail? There was no note.'

Steele was puzzled for a second. 'That's why I've came to see you. Not so much about the film, more about the actors, and one actress in particular. A certain Georgina McBride? Now she would win an Oscar, put her heart and soul – and a few other things – into her performance. All whilst wearing a tartan skirt that wouldn't spare Fran or Anna's blushes and very little else.'

'Poor Georgie,' Sanderson bowed his head, but it was clear to Steele that his grief at the mention of McBride's name was clearly false. 'Such a terrible shame. You got any leads?'

Again, Steele's brow furrowed and he shook his head slightly. Was this guy so blinkered to what was going on? 'Again, that's why I'm here to see you. Do you not think the two events, Ms McBride's murder, and us receiving this DVD are linked?'

'I wouldn't have thought so.' It was Sanderson's turn to shake his head. 'We're very select as to who we allow in.'

'Now we're getting somewhere.' Steele sat back in his chair. 'I need details, names.'

'I don't think so Detective Inspector,' Sanderson laughed. 'It still is Detective Inspector, isn't it Robert?'

'I'm not sure I like your tone Maurice!' Steele bawled. 'A woman has been murdered in a savage manner and as far as I can see you knew her intimately. You are therefore high on my list of suspects, and unless you co-operate fully I'll see that you're treated like every other manky scumbag we get down the station.'

Sanderson laughed again, a money laugh. There was no way a minion like Steele could come close. 'I hear you had young McCulloch in your sweaty grasp and he managed to elude you. I hear The Piazza was awash with uniformed officers at the time as well.' he raised a bushy eyebrow. 'Rather unfortunate that.'

'We're never likely to be on the same page are we?' Steele shook his head and sighed. 'Why do you fight for the forces of darkness? Something happen in childhood? The whole world against you? Better go and eat some worms?' Steele paused and leant forward on the oak desk, 'Or are you just a c...'

'Inspector!' Sanderson interrupted. 'If I didn't ensure that everyone,' he paused and leant forward himself, 'and I mean EVERYONE, got a fair trial then you buggers would have everyone in jail. Birmingham six? Guildford four? Ding dong the bells they are a ringing!'

'Garry McCulloch is a murderer, his cousin Alisdair a well known drug dealer and whoever killed Georgina McBride is a serious psychopath and if I were you I'd be worried. What if it's someone in your wee club? A wee touch of tinky winky envy? All of a sudden you're on our maniac's radar, would you talk to me then?' Steele sat back in his chair. 'Bet your bottom dollar you would, but would I listen? In the words of the great King Kenny "mibbee's aye, mibbees naw". Now could we start singing from the same hymn sheet?'

In his heart Sanderson knew he would always cooperate, it was the jousting he enjoyed with Steele. There were few like him, or few who liked him. He wasn't like the new drone detectives that Sanderson could wrap round his Masonic ring, the two of them were very alike in some respects – both determined to be right all the time. Sanderson couldn't remember a time when he was ever wrong, not in his recent history or cases. He sometimes felt he bent the truth badly to be right, but he was never wrong, never completely. 'What is it you want to know Robert?' he hissed. 'Is it names? I'll give you plenty of names, but I very much doubt I'll give you the name of the maniac who murdered sweet Georgie.'

Steele observed Sanderson as he licked his lips salaciously. Put a pervert in a suit and he's still a pervert, the same went for monkeys. He was losing his train of thought, he was sure he was going to be on the front foot with this one, that the catbird seat was his to look down from. He had forgotten how slippery Sanderson could be though, a moustachioed eel in a pinstriped suit. Steele could happily throw him back in the Cart where he had come from, no problem. One less defence lawyer wouldn't be a great loss to the world. No doubt another would rise from the primordial soup as soon as Sanderson breathed his last. Steele rolled his eyes, he wanted a drink, last night's alcohol had finally worn off. 'Names would be good Maurice,' he got out his notebook. 'As many as you like.' As he fished in his pockets for a pen, Maurice Sanderson reached across his desk and handed him his Parker. He then began to tell the detective inspector everything he had wanted to know.

13

The sun didn't set on the west end of Paisley, it had never made an appearance so it had no need to say goodbye. Weather was like that these days, just there and always dreich. The street lights on Wellmeadow Street flickered into life at eight forty-three and the bar RePUBlique de Madagascar was jumping. The RePUBlique de Madagascar was always jumping, for every nut in the west end it was the place to be. There were many and varied nuts in the West End, dealers, sleeping junkies, hustling pimps, sad eyed hookers, shakey jakeys and stoned students. No one just out for a quiet drink, Jesus no! If you weren't a wee bit wide before you entered through the doors of the RePUBlique de Madagascar then you better search for it somewhere in your arsenal, because being off kilter was a basic requirement to getting served. The music pumping from the two four-foot Tangent speakers at either end of the bar was reggae, heavy dub. It wasn't always heavy dub, but it was always reggae. Emmanuel Radisson McLeish made sure of that, and at six foot eight and as wide as the Clyde, very few in the bar disagreed with his music policy. Very few disagreed with any of the policies in the bar, there weren't any to disagree with. Everything and anything went.

Emmanuel sidled past Chantelle and reached for the lager pump, but as he was about to pull it back he noticed something out the corner of his eye. Someone by the unused dart board had pulled their works from the pocket of their jacket. 'Put your spoon away boy!' he boomed over the top of Dr Majika's clanging bass. 'You new here? Ya wanna do that g'won outside! Shoo! Shoo!' He motioned for the group of junkies to get into the yard and shoot up. 'You no do that in here!'

The Yard was a rat-infested cobbled back court that didn't belong to the pub, but was shared by the tenants of the tenement above the bar. If it technically didn't belong to the bar, or the bar owner (one Emmanuel Radisson McLeish), then whatever happened out there was (technically) nothing to do with him. The fact that he had discarded a couple of chairs and tables out the back that people could (technically) skin up on, shoot up on or shag on was (technically) nothing to do with him and he could keep getting his licence renewed by the council. He had friends there, friends with influence.

As the three junkies and their shared needle made their way out to the yard, Emmanuel poured a lager for himself. Red Stripe, none of that local bilge. As he was getting a head on his pint he felt a drip hit one of his dreadlocks. He ignored it, but when he felt a second, he looked to the ceiling. Water was coming through the light fitting.

The flat directly upstairs from the RePUBlique de Madagascar was swathed in darkness, the only light from the yellow lamppost directly outside. There was no sound other than the boom from the bar below. In the bathroom the shower was running, and had been doing so now for just over thirty hours. The pipe that the water cascaded down had become blocked with something and was backing up. The water from the shower had started lapping over the rim of the bath an hour ago and had ventured across the bare floorboards of the living room and to the front door. As the water made its way to the front door it had to negotiate Bob McLean, lying dead on the floor, his robe untied, exposing his small genitals and penis. He had soiled himself and three of his fingers had been roughly chopped from his right hand. The sun had gone down on Bob McLean a little over thirty hours ago.

14

Steele was distracted, the rain had all of a sudden began lashing down, hitting the window like a million tiny pebbles. He had been in the middle of relating to Mansell the details of the extensive list of people who were members of what Sanderson had laughingly called "Paisley's sexual elite". Steele had snorted at the thought and suggested to Sanderson that, having seen the best and worst Paisley had to offer, the "sexual elite" would be those who didn't have to wear the proverbial bag on their head during sex. As well as Sanderson and Georgina McBride, the list had thrown up a serious surprise, one Alisdair McCulloch and his now estranged wife Jean.

Mansell waited for Steele to come back to him, but he seemed transfixed by the rain. 'Anybody else of note?' he asked.

Steele turned his attention from the window. He rubbed at the back of his neck and grimaced. 'No, they seemed to be a very settled group, been doing it for years by all accounts, at first in and out of their own homes, but then they all stuck in a few quid and bought the site of The Renfrewshire Rope and Twine Co. last March for buttons, if you pardon the pun. I'm surprised that there's so many women involved in it.'

'You sound jealous boss,' laughed Mansell.

Steele raised an eyebrow. 'Of course I'm bloody jealous! Are you not?'

Mansell shrugged, 'Not really, can take it or leave it.'

'On the day this DVD was made there was apparently some character who had turned up with Georgina, which was unusual, but he didn't really fit in. He kept telling everyone he was into BDSM and feet...'

'Feet?' Mansell baulked.

'Feet,' Steele repeated with a frown. 'But by all accounts, he couldn't even raise a smile, just sat there in his pants like a spare one.'

'No name?' asked Mansell.

'Nope,' Steele scratched at his stubble. 'No names no pack drill. Middle aged man, bald as a coot, non-descript. According to Sanderson he doesn't appear in any of the film, so it would seem he's our budding Steven Spielberg. Why? I don't know.'

'Do you think he's our killer?' asked Mansell. 'Or just a run of the mill blackmailer?'

'A run of the mill blackmailer,' Steele smiled. 'I like that. I don't know what he's up to, there was no note to Sanderson. Maybe he's biding his time. Can't see him being our killer though, he was as bald as a billiard ball.' He nodded in a knowing manner to his assistant.

Mansell was clueless, and shrugged. 'So?'

'So?' Steele raised one eyebrow. 'According to Kapoor, our killer has a thick mane of blond hair. Did you forget?'

The recognition clunked on Mansell's face.

'You want to read your own notes now and again.' Steele told him. 'So, as far as we know he's going to turn out to be a blackmailer, but then again, maybe he knows our killer and he's blackmailing him.'

'Alisdair McCulloch?' asked Mansell.

Steele pursed his lips and made a long farting noise. 'Can't see it,' he shook his head. 'Maybe one of his acolytes, but I can't see him getting personally involved. Would be a helluva of coincidence, him *and* his cousin committing two separate murders on the same day.'

'He's not a blondie either.' Added Mansell.

'True,' sighed Steele. 'Maybe we should look at the film again, see if it throws up anything.'

'Do we have to?' scowled Mansell.

'We'll send it down to forensic instead,' suggested Steele. 'Let their minds get poisoned.'

'That's a better idea. It's way too early in the morning for any kind of perversion.' Mansell acquiesced.

15

Blair Devine was having trouble focussing on his breakfast. Muesli? He was old enough to remember when it had first come to these shores in the early seventies. What the West of Scotland had in common with Switzerland he had no idea. Why then should we share their diet instead of feeding it to rabbits, as any self-respecting Scotsman should. *Give me a roll on square sausage wuman! And remember to dip the roll in the chip pan!* That's what he should be saying to Belinda, but he didn't have the necessary balls. He had learned that the hard way.

'Something wrong with your cereal dear?' she scowled. Her breakfast consisted of a cup of strong coffee and a menthol cigarette, king size. Nothing more. She needed nothing more, Blair eschewed, she had bugger all to do all day apart from sit about on her fat arse and watch the cleaner clean, gin and bitter lemon in hand. Bitter was right. She'd turned that way immediately after returning from their honeymoon. She had been happy with Blackpool then, but as the years wore on (twenty-eight and still counting), her demands increased. Spain, The Canaries, The Algarve, Singapore, Australia, Florida, a world cruise. After the cruise he had laughed that he had better get saving for the trip to the moon. Her face cracked not a jot. In her eyes he was the provider and her role was to keep house and look after the family. "The family" consisted of one son – Ralph, but since his teenage years he had insisted on being referred to as Raif, like he was some posh film star. Belinda had encouraged him to express himself in this manner, and the two of them looked at Blair pitifully as he said, "Oh aye, just like the football team - Raith Rovers". He had laughed, but the scorn in the room was tangible.

All his life she treated Ralph like her wee angel, instead of what he had wanted from a son – a rough and ready rascal – but it wasn't to be. Much to his mother's delight he "came out" at his twenty first birthday party (which Blair had paid through the nose for). Belinda was delighted and Blair did his best to feign surprise, even though he probably knew before his son what his sexual predilections were going to be. He then introduced Marcus to the assembled company as the love of his life (after his mother, of course). Marcus didn't last long, neither did Peter, John, David, Brian, Paul or Alexander. His son was a selfish bastard and unless a partner revered him twenty-four hours a day there was no future in the relationship. Selfish and tight, that was his son Ralph, that's why the bugger still lived at home at the age of twenty-eight. It wasn't that he didn't have the money, he'd been a trolley dolly for nigh on three and a half years now, and for the five before that he was a management accountant, fully qualified. And not one penny in digs had been handed over in all that time! Blair raged at Belinda about it every now and again, but like every other thing he raged about, it was pointless. Her wee boy didn't need to pay them a thing and it would break her heart if he left. There were three of them in the relationship, and he knew exactly where he fitted in – the mug working night and day to pay for everything!

'No, it's fine,' he pushed the plate in front of him, 'just not that hungry. Is that today's paper?'

Belinda was reading the Paisley Daily Express, flicking through the small ads and deaths. 'No, it's...' she looked at the top of the page, 'Monday's. Here.' She slid it across the breakfast bar towards him.

It just stopped short and Blair had to reach to grab it. As he lifted it towards him it trailed through his cereal and consequently on to his trousers. Ralph chose that moment to enter the kitchen.

'Oh Father,' he shook his head. 'Bit of a continence issue is it?' He kissed his mother on the cheek. 'I think just French toast this morning,' and patted his stomach. 'Watching my figure before everybody else does.' He laughed falsely and sat at the breakfast bar on the stool Belinda had vacated to see to her pride and joy's breakfast. There was a time when Blair would have scowled and commented at the way he treated his mother, but now he didn't care, the two of them deserved each other. 'What comic's that you're reading anyway Pater dearest?'

'Local rag,' he sorted the pages and held the front page in front of himself. He quickly scanned it and the details of the grisly murder less than a mile from their home. He felt his muesli come back up on him slightly. 'I don't believe it!'

'What's that Father?' chirped Ralph. 'Paisley dragged itself into the twenty-first century with the opening of a gay bar?' Ralph and his mother shared a look and a smile.

'Eh? What?' Blair stuttered, his eyes trying to take in all the details. He turned the page and continued reading. 'For fu...' he carried on reading. 'This is too much of a coincidence. Pass me the phone?' he asked Belinda.

Belinda threw him a look of scorn. 'What did your last slave die of?' She carried on whisking the eggs for her son's breakfast and made no attempt to pass him the phone that was within her reach.

He was tempted to say he'd beat her to death with the handset of a phone for being cheeky, but he knew better. 'I can't believe they're being so stupid!' he rose from his stool and crossed the kitchen towards the phone.

'Maybe they've been taking lessons from you,' Belinda quipped instantly, sharing another look with her son. 'What are you babbling on about anyway? Is your first lesson not at half past?'

'Never mind that.' He carried the phone back over to the breakfast bar, dialling Directory Enquiries as he did so. 'Mill Street Police station, Paisley please.'

Belinda and Ralph fell silent and both looked with mouths open at Blair as he waited to be put through to the police. 'Yes,' he said as calmly as he could. 'I don't know who I should speak to, but I think I know who the killer of the lawyer Georgina McBride might be.' His eyes focussed on the paper in front of him, two stories on the same day and they had put two and two together and got five. He was put through to someone and had to say who he was, where he lived, everything before he could even start with his story. All the while his wife and son were unusually quiet.

Blair Devine had been a driving instructor for twenty-nine-years, it had been the only job he had ever wanted to do and most of the time he loved it, the open road, the freedom, the challenge of getting people through their test, the way they smiled like maniacs on their first few lessons. Every now and again, however, the job threw up what he had learned to call his cash cows. Learners who were inexplicably rubbish at taking any sort of direction, and who didn't appear to enjoy driving, yet they kept coming back, week after week and paying their money. Why they didn't just give up was beyond him. Of course, he never once suggested this. Why would you?

Harry Spencer had been one such "cash cow". He just kept coming back, time after time after time, cash in hand and head filled with mince. Instead of listening to the instructions he told Blair all about his life, the ups and downs. At the end, there were mainly downs – money getting tight, relationships getting strained to the point of snapping, custody battles, a tenacious lawyer called Georgina McBride taking him for everything he had until he had nothing, save some money from his credit union account that he was using to fund his driving lessons. It was only when he saw her grainy photo in the paper that he realised she was the same woman he had encountered at The Renfrewshire Rope & Twine Co. He gulped and his eyes rolled in his head. He had stopped teaching Harry Spencer when the money had ran out, he had sent him for his test twice, but he had an understanding with the examiners. A wink and a nod and a palm greased ensured that the "cash cows" just kept giving. He remembered the day Harry finally ran out of money, Blair actually felt awful, with the other "cash cows" the money NEVER ran out, there was never any need to look into their eyes as you abandoned the tortured puppy.

He related everything he knew about Harry Spencer and expected to be told to hang on while they sent round a squad car and a S.W.A.T. team. He felt, after all, that if Spencer had started on some killing spree, it wouldn't be long until he realised how much B.D.S.M. (Blair Devine School of Motoring) had shafted him and that he wanted to reap his revenge. He was told the information would be passed on and thanked for his help and cooperation.

'But...' he stammered. 'Is that it? Are you not going to...'? The line had fallen silent, and right on cue his wife and son began babbling. All at once he was the centre of attention.

16

'Got away with it again, eh?' Mansell checked the mirror and negotiated a lane change on the one-way system at Gilmour Street train station.

Steele was shoving a cheese savoury into his mouth and spluttered, 'What do you mean, *again*?' Pieces of soggy pastry hit the dashboard.

Much to his chagrin, Mansell pulled a cloth from the side of the door and wiped the offending detritus. Waiting for Steele to do so would be like waiting for hell to freeze over. He was a dirty big sod, but no matter how many times he was told he didn't listen. 'Well,' Mansell tried not to sound judgemental. 'I know you lamped that lassie in the Post Office,' he paused as he stopped the car and put it into neutral at the traffic lights outside the Sheriff Court. 'You know you lamped her, she knows you lamped her. Christ! I'm sure even Bain's certain you lamped her.'

Steele cleared his throat. 'Enough with the "lamping" would you? You make me sound like a monster. It was a reflex reaction, and one that I regret, but. And as they say in all the best porn films, "and it's a big but", it's not my fault if the CCTV in the Post Office wasn't working. Don't you see a pattern emerging here? All this crap about CCTV making it safer to sleep in your bed at night and there's not one of the fucking things switched on. Somebody, somewhere is making an absolute fortune out of doing sweet F.A., and we've all fell for it.'

Mansell tried his best not to laugh, but the smile on his face gave him away. 'Regardless,' he started. 'You got away with it. You'd fall drunk into the Cart and come out sober with a salmon supper.'

'Fair point,' Steele stuffed the last of the pastry into his mouth and muttered. 'I got away with it.'

They were on their way to Ferguslie, to the home of Alisdair McCulloch. They knew there was no way he'd cooperate, (grassing was grassing was grassing) but Steele felt it would be good to let him know that he knew he fitted into the equation somewhere. People, criminals especially, acted differently when they felt they were being watched. They were more likely to slip up, give themselves away. The drove in silence down Caledonia Road, left into Clark street, then up Greenhills, past the stadium and into Ferguslie on Park Avenue. In Darkwood Crescent they were confronted by something they had no way of anticipating.

'What in the name of God is he doing?' asked Mansell.

'It's them that's doing things in the name of God.' Steele replied. 'It's been a while since I was last in Ferguslie, but I don't remember anything like this before.'

'It's new to me as well sir.'

The car was brought to a halt by a man of about twenty-four, wearing a track suit that was mainly black in colour, but was decorated with red, yellow and green. The cannabis leaf emblem on the front of the top gave him away. He was a crazy stoner dancing in front of a choir of Born Agains in anoraks and long coats. They were singing like linties, praising the Great God almighty, but were being forced to raise their singing voices almost as high as the heavens as the track-suited man had turned his ghetto blaster up to max and his choice of music wasn't sitting too well with them and their Born Again ears. A crowd of half a dozen youths stood by watching the show, pointing and laughing.

Steele wound down the window and was about to display his warrant card when he recognised the tune the man was playing to the choir. He then took more note of the stoner's dancing. He was gyrating back and forward, hands on someone's invisible hips, pumping the air to Judge Dredd's Big Seven. 'Marvellous!' Steele boomed to Mansell. 'Switch off the engine, I want to hear this.' He got out the car and stretched his arms over his head as the stoner directed his thrustings at a particularly prim female member of the choir. Steele laughed out loud as one of the male members, sporting casual beige flannels and an olive tank-top went to her assistance and began to shout erratically at the dancer. The stoner continued unabashed, thrusting at the male now with fake lust in his eyes as the song came to its conclusion.

'And I'll call the police!' was the words Steele heard as the music stopped. The stoner simply laughed at him as the next song started to blare from his stereo. The man in the tank-top stooped to try and stop the music but the speed with which the man in the tracksuit moved visibly surprised him, catching his wrist with a firm grasp. He backed off, his head shaking with a mix of fear and fury that threatened to topple his toupee.

Steele thought again about getting his warrant card out, but decided to wait for the next track. Seconds of grumbling were replaced and drowned out by 36D by The Beautiful South, and as the choir raised their voices the stoner raised his hands and made gestures to suggest he was squeezing his large breasts, his face seemingly aching with desire, hips thrusting erratically. Steele laughed out loud. Too loud for the The Tank-Top who shot him a scowl as he pulled a mobile phone from his pocket. Steele saw him mouth the words *police please* and took his cue and walked straight up to him, warrant card in hand. He quickly flashed it and just as quickly replaced it in his pocket.

'How can I help you sir?' his tone was business-like.

The Tank-Top looked stunned, muttering inaudibly into the phone before switching it off and replacing it in the pocket of his beige flannels. He then mouthed some words that Steele failed to recognise.

'I'M SORRY SIR, YOU'RE GOING TO HAVE TO SPEAK UP!' He was face to face, noses almost touching. Steele could hear him slightly, a Northern Irish accent, barking like a dog about God. There were pockets of evangelistic groups popping up in Paisley every day, mostly northern Irish or African. The Godless hole was having an awful lot of religion rammed down its throat. Steele had no time for any of it.

The man backed off, wiping his cheek were stray spit had landed. He shook his head forcefully and began. 'THIS FILTHY PERVERT HAS...'

Just then the stoner switched off the music, instantly making him feel embarrassed at the words coming out of his mouth. The crowd of youths around them laughed heartily. He stretched his neck out, an angry tortoise coming out of hibernation. 'He,' he pointed, 'has been playing filthy and suggestive songs and I want you to charge him.'

'With what?' asked Steele.

The man's face was a picture of confusion, eyes questioning, mouth open. 'I don't know,' he scowled indignantly.

'Well sir,' Steele held up his hands. 'In any other circumstances I would be within my rights to charge him with breach of the peace...'

'Yes yes,' the man nodded autistically.

'But!' Steele paused, a grin forming on his lips, 'Then I would have to charge every one of you with the same crime.'

Shock and awe. 'This is ridiculous!' the man fumed. 'We are The Church of The Beloved Nazarene. We have a right to...'

'And this gentleman,' Steele pointed to the stoner who was picking up his bike, 'is, I'm assuming a resident of Ferguslie and therefore has the right to act accordingly. And if that means playing his own hymns at the same time...'

'STOP HIM!' The Tank-Top raged at him. 'HE'S GETTING AWAY!'

Steele turned and watched as the man cycled away uneasily, the ghetto blaster unbalancing his mountain bike. 'Carry on with your singing sir and I hope the Lord shines on you.' He said earnestly. 'Thank you for using our service and if you have any problems with the way in which we dealt with your complaint please feel free to make a complaint to our Mill Street station. I'm Detective Sergeant McGlaughlin and my colleague in the car is DS Patterson, pleasure to meet you. Carry on,' he added cheerfully as he walked back to the car.

The two men shared a happy silence as the car continued on its way to McCulloch's residence. The local neighbourhood drug baron prided himself in that he still lived in the community he served. He had tried living elsewhere, in the more salubrious surroundings of Elderslie, but had failed to realise the value of The Golfing Pound. Every time trouble turned up on his doorstep, the police weren't too far behind. The police took note when something untoward happened in places like Elderslie, but in Ferguslie Park you could stand naked in your window every Friday and Saturday night touting for business and no one would bat an eyelid, no jaws would drop. He was back in Ferguslie after only four months, moving into a new build semi and making his next-door neighbour an offer he couldn't refuse to sell their house to him. The offer was well over the odds as to what the property was worth, no violence was involved, he was Alisdair McCulloch, a businessman not a barbarian. At least he was now.

'You can buy anything but class,' Mansell muttered as he turned the car into McCulloch's three lane drive. There were no other cars on it.

'I would say that the cupboard's bare,' Steele slammed the car door shut loudly enough to wake the dead. He failed to register the look Mansell threw in his direction. He walked to the front door and noticed one of the blinds upstairs was shaking as though recently peered through. He battered loudly on the oak panel before pressing the doorbell.

DING! DING! DING! DING! It echoed in the empty hallway, but found a resting place in Steele's head. 'Simply the best,' his mouth sang the Tina Turner song, his brain unconscious of what he was doing. He hated the song, but smiled at McCulloch's audacity. He looked at Mansell. He was shaking his head at the garishness of the garden, marble ornaments he expected only to be found in the windows of tacky amusement arcades and an army of gnomes, cats and sleeping cherubs. It amused Steele to see Mansell turn up his nose at the way most people lived, if he could shake that condescension from his disposition he would make a fine policeman. It was a good job the gates had been closed, Steele thought, or the good taste detective would have noticed they were miniatures of the gates to Ibrox stadium, the lions indicative of the welcome that lay ahead. He hammered the door again and listened for signs of life within. He quickly looked up at the window where the blinds had been moving before and saw them flutter again. He knew McCulloch wasn't the kind to shy away from a fight, so he shouted through the letterbox. 'Police! Can you open up! I know you're in there!' Unsure as to whom he was shouting at. He waited a couple of minutes before waving at the tutting Mansell to start the car. 'Let's go before the natives get restless.'

17

As Steele left The Tile Bar in Smithill Street he pulled his collar round him. The wind was squally, tearing through the gap between the Abbey and the town hall and down the narrow street. Steele, who was used to drinking his own body weight, had taken it easy, not feeling the need to bolt his drinks like he had when he had first stopped smoking. Maybe he was finally conquering the poisonous weed. He allowed a smile to cross his face as he turned into Central Way and towards the taxi rank. Central Way was nothing more than an enclosed bus stop, the canopy provided by the floor of the Piazza car park. It was empty save for some pigeons flying erratically from one perch to another. All the days' buses had come and gone. Paisley was a Ghost town after seven in the evening, no matter the season. It was a town slowly and visibly crumbling into a heap. It would soon be just dust scattered in the squally wind. Steele wondered if the decline of Pompeii started with the opening of shops that sold just tat that retailed for a pound. He almost laughed out loud, and lurching into his pocket, found some change. He pulled it out and tried to examine it in the half-light. The next thing he knew the coins were strewn into the air, his eyes passing them on the way down to the hard pavement. Confusion was quickly followed by a searing pain at the back of his head. His nose was the first part of his body to hit the ground and the last thing he saw was a pair of shiny white trainers running quickly away. He tried to remain conscious long enough to see more of the person who had hit him, but his brain slumped into blackness and his mouth felt as though it had been filled with all the dust of Pompeii.

18

He wondered if he had laughed out loud and childishly placed his hand over his mouth to stop himself in case the urge came over him again. Not that anyone would hear him downstairs, his wife and sons were still away, possibly for good, he wasn't sure. More and more he had been coming to the loft, just to think, no, he almost laughed again. He knew exactly why he was here, to gloat, to re-enact, to revel. He stood over the disused scalextric track, it had been over two years since it had been plugged in. He considered switching it on, but he was way too wired even for that simple pleasure. He left it to the dust and turned his face to the skylight.

It was genius. Pure and simple. All these people, these so-called professionals getting in his way, making him feel stupid, making him a laughing stock, it was genius. What he was doing to them. Who looked stupid now? The lawyer with her cut tongue, the tool of her trade? Did she look down her nose at him now? Did she snigger when he left the room? The reporter with his severed fingers? Would he write another word that made him embarrassed? Stupid? Ridiculous? A laughing stock amongst his peers?

He wasn't stupid, he wasn't typical, he told himself. People who did what he did (and let's face it, he was doing it now, was he a serial killer yet? He wasn't sure how many you needed to bump off to gain that tag.) usually took trophies, trinkets to help them remember what they'd done and get their jollies from it at a later date. Jesus! How could they forget what they had done? He had every second of both killings playing on repeat in the cinema of his brain. How he analysed it, how he would have done things differently, used different locations, different tactics, and on and on. He dissected them thoroughly, so that next time would be perfectly clean. That was the genius of it all, he hadn't really planned any of it, not at all. He had went along to do it, no doubt about that, but he hadn't thought through exactly how. and all the tiny details in between. It was instinctive. It was genius. He was genius. He felt his hand slip into his trousers. He hadn't even noticed himself getting hard. Who was next? He knew who, but tried to block the vision of her face from his head. Angie. Angie, Angie, Angie, the cause of all this, he thought of her from behind, it was the only way he could, he couldn't look into those scheming eyes, her hair almost to her arse. He envisaged her bending over – a pram of all things – and knew exactly what part of her to tear. He tried to hold it back, tried to find something else, but he couldn't stop, not now. The Scalextric track didn't just have dust on it now. It had genius.

19

The pitch black of his father's eyes, panda-like, bore into his own like laser beams. His mouth didn't speak, didn't have to, he knew what he was saying – people from our background didn't join the police force, they were the enemy, have you learned nothing son? That picture of his father spoke more than a million words, but the one that was writ large was not pride, but disappointment. Serious betrayal was afoot as far as his father was concerned. How could he hold his head up in the club now, amongst the other former miners? He could almost hear their whispers already and he hadn't even graduated. It would be all over the village, he was too old to move but he didn't want to live with the shame. It had always been us and them, and now his son, his one and only was now one of them.

Black. Pitch black. He felt his mouth trying to open and take in air, but nothing. Only the filth of the dirty pavement wanted in, strangling his windpipe. It was just dark, but it seemed to be swirling and getting lighter. He could feel something at his arm, a rocking on his bicep. Amid the rocking he started to smile internally, no longer trying to get up, he was happy, happier than Larry. He felt himself smile like he had never done since childhood. Hats off to Larry! He was almost howling, nearly delirious. He felt his whole body go limp, the stress and tightness of his life, releasing into the darkness and disappearing. Now it was white. Brilliant Antarctic white, the brightness of which he had never seen before. Glowing like a million-watt bulb straight into the back of his eyelids. The light was inside him, coming from inside him. He heard himself laugh, he heard himself sing. Hats off to Larry, he crooned drunkenly. He felt the rocking, the constant movement from his arm. Back and forward, Hats off to Larry! Back and forward. Are you okay? Back and forward. Hats off to…That's him in the recovery position. No more rocking. Hats off... Is he saying something? He's coming round. Hats. Hats. Hats...

'You're okay mate,' a voice in the darkness laughed. 'What's that all about man? "Hats, hats" He's pure steaming by the way.'

'There's an ambulance coming,' a different voice, female, nasal, junkie-esque, 'just you lie still. You got anything?'

He felt hands in his pockets, his trousers, his jacket, even his back pocket. It was like a snake was crawling over him. He was getting robbed by a snake.

'Fuck's sake!'

'What is it?'

'He's a polis. Look,'

'Bolt.' Voices getting further away. He hadn't opened his eyes and had no intention of doing so. He wanted to get back to the brilliant whiteness, but knew he wouldn't, he was coming round. Slowly, but he was coming round, the marvellous brilliant white was nowhere to be seen.

20

'You were lucky,' The nurse smiled and ticked off something in his chart.

'How do you figure that one out?' he caught the glint in her eye. 'Some chancer clocks me with a baseball bat and then I'm robbed by the junkie equivalent of Bonnie and Clyde. Remind me to put the lottery on this week.'

'Aye,' she replaced the chart at the end of his bed. 'But at least they phoned an ambulance.'

'Suppose,' Steele agreed begrudgingly.

'You need rest,' she walked towards the next bed, the patient, a pensioner toothless and asleep, dribbling down his craggy cheek. 'At least another night.'

'We'll see.' He felt the patch of bandage on the back of his head and flinched. He did feel lucky, not a feeling he often experienced, but this bump on the head might just have done him the world of good. God, he caught himself, he sounded like his mother. He looked around the ward, six beds - all full of men older than he was, sicker than he was, less conscious than he was. Drips were the order of the day, and he felt glad, nay lucky, that he wasn't attached to one. The clock on the far wall was striking twenty past six and as he turned and faced the window he saw that the sun was nowhere to be seen, on holiday on the other side of the planet. He felt the cannula on his hand before he saw it, scratching and catching against the taut stained linen. He held up the back of his hand and examined it. As he did the nurse, who was now shifting down to the end bed chided him silently. 'What's this for?' he mouthed towards her.

She began walking towards him, the soles of her shoes squawking like a two mating gulls. 'Leave it in,' she instructed him. 'You're not out the woods yet, you never know when we might have need of a sedated detective.' The smirk on her face warmed Steele's heart. There was a fallacy about the nursing profession and the police hitting it off romantically simply due to the nature of their shift patterns. In his experience the opposite was true. A few furtive dalliances with disinterested nurses over the twenty odd years of his police career teaching him never to trust a cliché. Or a nurse for that matter!

'I could think of a few I'd like sedated,' Steele responded, shifting to a sitting position in the bed.

The nurse instinctively sorted the pillows behind his back. 'There'll be a tea round in about five minutes.'

'Good,' Steele sat back against the pillows. 'My tongue feels like sandpaper.'

'Have some water,' she nodded to the other side of the bed and the full jug and empty plastic glass on top of the bedside cabinet.

Steele eyed the full jug gratefully, still becoming accustomed to his surroundings. 'Cheers.' The nurse walked back down the ward, silently apart from her squawking shoes. As she did so Steele poured the room temperature water from the jug lustily. He would have rather it was ice cold, but beggars cannot be choosers. He smirked, some water almost spilling out the glass. A cliché that he trusted. He guzzled two glasses of the water before he was sated, but poured himself another one to sip on, knowing his thirst had only temporarily left the building. He looked around the small ward with more clarity than he had when he'd first woken, searching out the toilet. He saw the unmarked door in the corner next to another patient's bed and rose from his own to make his way to it. The nurse glared at him, but her expression softened when he pointed to the toilet, indicating that this was where he was heading. As he straightened himself up beside the bed he made sure his backside wouldn't be exposed through his blue hospital gown. He could see down the corridor where a young uniformed officer was idly leaning on the nurses' desk, probably offering his services as a Romeo. He would learn, Steele grimaced. Suddenly, the manoeuvre from bed to standing caused excruciating pain in his head. He quickly sat back down again – he had no choice.

'Are you okay?' the nurse was back by his side.

'Not particularly,' he lay back gingerly.

She checked the back of his head. 'It'll be like that for a few days,' she told him. 'Your stitches are still intact, but I'll get you a couple of paracetamol for the pain.'

'Can you get me something else as well?' he asked.

Her questioning eyes suddenly remembered where he had been heading when he had been stopped in his tracks. 'I'll just get you something from the sluice,' she smiled.

21

Dave Mansell shook his head and cursed his luck. Of all the days for Steele to go AWOL! He'd tried his phone – dead, his house – locked up and empty, all over Mill Street (the canteen got a thorough going over) – nothing. He had vanished into thin air, and here he was, hanging out a first floor window overlooking Well Street gasping for some fresh air.

There had been an anonymous tip-off to the council that the place was flooding, and when their workers had finally got the door open they were met with the sight of a dead and naked Bob McLean. The first three fingers of his right hand had been roughly hacked at and left at the scene. 'Guess he won't be making the old Boy Scout salute anymore,' John McGlaughlin had laughed upon entering the dismal flat.

Mansell scowled at him but didn't bother to correct him. The Boy Scout's saluted with their left hand, at least they did in his day.

'You're Dad not with you?' Patterson, the other John had chided. 'Heard he's pulled a sickie.'

'Probably lying in his own pish somewhere,' McGlaughlin had added.

Mansell knew their bravado would be seriously muted if Steele were here, but again he kept quiet about it. It was after all a murder scene. Solemnity and calm were called for, not schoolyard japes and rugby club backslapping. He had let them have their five minutes of fun, before opening a window and hanging his head out.

McGlaughlin was assuming command, he outranked Mansell insofar as he had been at Mill Street longer. He'd let it go this time, confrontation never having been his strong suit.

Mansell pulled himself back from the open window and, popping a mint in his mouth, he surveyed the scene. He couldn't help but stare at Bob McLean's flabby cadaver, his pallid skin heavy and wrinkled like rhino's, hair like shredded wheat, limbs untouched by any gym workout. He mused for a second – the dead McLean looked almost the same as he did in life, all that was missing was the cackle. He imagined his lungs, black as the Earl of Hell's waistcoat. If he hadn't had been murdered the lungs were bound to get him sooner rather than later. He assumed it would be little consolation to the dead reporter as he wandered noiselessly around his bleak flat. There was nothing to it, just stuff – basic furniture, cracked tiles, flaking wallpaper, matted carpets with more cigarette burns than material, barely a drop of food and dirty clothes and bed clothes. Mansell totted up, he'd probably been a reporter for at least thirty years – where were the trappings of wealth? Where were the photographs of past glories? Where was the sense of achievement? Nowhere. Everything Bob McLean had ever earned seemed to have gone towards destroying either his liver or his lungs, and he hadn't even managed that – a knock on the head had done for him, followed by the severing of fingers, strangely still left at the scene. Mansell had read enough American crime fiction and CIA reports to know that serial killers where famed for their trophies. But with this one and Georgina McBride's tongue? That had been an attempt at trophy collecting, an afterthought almost. And now this, the trophy fingers left behind at the scene? Had he been disturbed, or, as Mansell suspected, was he just making it up as he went along? It was clear it was the same perpetrator, the M.O. was too similar. What was it about though? Who or what linked Bob McLean and Georgina McBride? Looking back at McLean's corpse Mansell found it hard to imagine The Renfrewshire Rope and Twine Co. was the tie that bound them. He laughed out loud, Jesus! Had he been around Steele too long, making crap jokes and laughing at them. What was it Steele had said Sanderson had called them, "Paisley's sexual elite" or some such nonsense. It was hard to imagine McLean fitting into that scenario. He took his eyes off the corpse for a moment and at the actions of

McGlaughlin and Patterson as they chatted conspiratorially. He didn't like the look of it. They were making decisions, jumping to conclusions more like. At the same time as they left the flat clutching their mobiles, Mansell's vibrated in his pocket. The screen read MILL ST, it would be a hungover, and hopefully contrite Steele with some cock and bull story as to his no show.

'This had better be good ya big lush,' he answered.

'Eh, Detective Sergeant Mansell?' a female voice spoke.

Mansell recognised the lilt and blushed instantly. It was Mhairi MacKay. 'Sorry Mhairi, I was expecting a call from someone else.'

'Detective Inspector Steele?' she asked softly, softly like she had some news, not good news.

'Yes, why?'

'Well he's in hospital,' she told him. 'He was attacked last night.'

'Is he all right?' Mansell feared the worst. 'How is he?'

'He's fine,' she replied. 'Doesn't quite sound like his old self though.'

Mansell was relieved. 'You mean he sounds like a normal human being, like the rest of us?'

They shared a laugh. 'He wants you to go and see him, take clothes up to him. He says he's going to discharge himself, but his clothes are in a state.'

'No problem Mhairi,' Mansell said to her. 'Anything else?'

'Ward twenty-seven, sixth floor.' She said abruptly, the line then going dead. It was like she had been caught using the telephone when she was supposed to be doing something else. Mansell remembered what it was like to be in uniform, everybody looking at you. Not just the general public, everyone at the station as well.

He headed for the door and passed the uniformed officer at the door, he appeared to be awaiting instructions. 'The two John's appear to have it all wrapped up,' he told him. 'I'm out of here, too many cooks and all that.'

At the bottom of the close McGlaughlin and Patterson stopped talking when they saw him. 'If you guys have got this sussed I've other fish to fry.' He opened the close door and the two detectives let it slowly close over before they started talking again. Mansell watched through the small window before waving to them and walking under the To-Let sign attached to the closed down Co-op supermarket to where his car was parked. He got in the car and headed for the hospital.

22

Blair Devine didn't like sitting in the test centre waiting. The waiting was the worst. His latest cash cow – Jadine Anderson, a dippy overweight blond of twenty-eight – was taking her test with Arthur Bale (Bale the Fail) and Blair was in no doubt she'd come back in tears and he'd have to drive her home. Again! Reassuring her again that it was just nerves, and that she was capable – on her day – of passing the test. No question. He had the patter down to a tee, knew exactly which buttons to push to get them to return to him, and not seek out a different driving instructor to assist them with their abysmal driving skills.

He had booked her in for the first two lessons of the day – double bubble. From eight forty five to ten forty five she had been shocking, mounting a kerb in Potterhill whilst trying to reverse the car around a corner. She had almost crossed lanes and battered into a bus on the Linwood to St James' dual carriageway. She had been distracted by a landing 737 and Blair had hauled at the steering wheel to correct her action. After that she had suggested that she needed a drink to calm her nerves. Blair had shaken his head, reminding her of the drink driving laws. They had shared a laugh, you had to keep your cash cows sweet, it didn't do to treat them the way you wanted to. It was all an act. His whole life. His whole life was just an act. His marriage, his work. It was all a sham for which he had no real feeling and he no longer cared. He did it all out of habit.

He sat looking at the other three instructors awaiting the return of their students. Only one, a newly qualified female instructor, a bottle blond fifty-year-old who sported the moniker Pass With Pammy, was the only one looking nervous. The other two, both older than himself, had the thousand-yard stare of someone who didn't care one way or the other whether their students came back in one piece or not. Blair regretted naming the company

BDSM every day of the week. It had been a long time ago, before sexual deviance permeated every corner of the television. Back then only the hardcore deviants knew what bondage and sadomasochism were. Now the name of his company was established – he had a three inch square ad in The Yellow Pages! - and he got plenty of repeat business and recommendations. He was loathed to change it just to follow fashion, the one trick ponies could stick their quirky and hilarious name up their exhausts.

He took his phone from his pocket and turned up the volume, he'd had it on vibrate through the lesson, feeling sure that the wooden tops at Mill Street would contact him at some time to ask about Harry Spencer and to offer him protection until Spencer was apprehended and safely behind bars. He looked at the screen, there had been no calls. He could see his hand shake as it held the phone, no matter how hard he tried, he couldn't get Spencer out of his head. He was sure he'd be on his list of people who'd "done him over", no doubt, and had hardly slept a wink since he'd seen Monday's Express. He had lain awake listening to every creak and stretch of the floorboards, the whirr of the fridge freezer and the strange scuttling from the loft – probably just a wood louse, but late at night everything was magnified. Of course, Belinda had slept right through as usual, her face mask and hair net saving her from the things that went bump in the night.

He put the phone back in his pocket and wandered over to the window. He saw his car pull into the car park and checked his watch. Five minutes early – she must have really screwed up! Poor cow. He watched as Jadine switched off the engine, got out of the car and pulled up the bonnet. Bale got out, clipboard in hand and swept his hand through his hair before pointing to the engine and asking her something. He ticked the paper on the clipboard and asked another question. He asked, he ticked. He asked, he ticked. Jadine put down the bonnet and the two of them made their way back into the car.

Blair watched silently out the window as Bale got out the passenger side, quickly followed by Jadine on the driver's side. She ran round the front of the car and hugged him clumsily, clutching in her hand her pass certificate. Blair's jaw dropped. How could this be? He'd greased Bale's palm, crossed it with much more than silver. The bastard! He had calculated that having Jadine as a student brought in nearly two hundred and fifty pounds every month. How was he going to replace that? His head dropped onto the window sill and he sighed audibly.

'I passed Blair!' he heard the voice behind him and struggled to get his head off the sill. 'I passed! Can you believe it?'

He turned and looked into the eyes of his overjoyed student. 'That's brilliant,' he lied. 'See, I told you you had it in you.'

As she ran to him and hugged him, he caught sight of Bale in the doorway and mouthed at him "What the fuck?".

Bale simply shrugged and mouthed back, "she was good".

Jadine released him from her grip. 'I suppose I'll be driving myself back home?' she jangled the keys in front of him.

Blair was confused and distraught. 'Eh, aye, I suppose you will. I just need to have a word with the examiner a minute. You go down and start the car.'

'Brilliant!' she bounced off towards the stairwell.

Blair entered the examiner's office and fifty pounds in tenners was swiftly thrust into his hand. 'What happened Arthur? What the...'

'I couldn't do it Blair,' he shook his head. 'She was good, drove perfectly.'

'You're joking!' Blair put the money in his wallet and put it in his pocket. 'She was that bad in her last lesson I had considered not paying you. She nearly killed me.'

Arthur Bale held the door open for him and again shrugged. 'She was good.'

Blair was slowly simmering to the boil as he walked to the car. His mood wasn't helped by Jadine waving and smiling at him like a maniac. 'In you get Blair.' She beeped the horn. Toot, toot.

'Fucking toot, toot,' Blair muttered. 'Probably gave him a gammy! "she was good" "she was good". Aye, good at what?'

'What's that?' Jadine asked.
'Nothing,' Blair shook his head. 'Just thinking out loud.'

Blair's mood didn't change as she spluttered every gear change and stalled at every junction on the way home. The rancid smell from the tannery at the traffic lights on Mill Street didn't help either as she again stalled before jumping the lights as they turned from green to red. As the car passed the new flats next to the police station he had made up his mind to get out at the next set of traffic lights and force her into the passenger seat. Something he saw made him change his mind though. Something he saw made his whole mood swing from black to bright rainbow colours. The thing he saw was the sight of Harry Spencer being marched – handcuffed – into Mill Street police station by detectives McGlaughlin and Patterson. The Two Johns were confident they had got their man.

23

It felt strange for Mansell to see Steele look so vulnerable. The big man was normally a tower, nothing could touch him, but as he looked through the window to the prone figure sitting on the chair by the bed in his hospital gown, a lump developed in his throat. Steele caught sight of him and beckoned him to come in.

Mansell followed his nose, the place was honking. He looked at the grey figures in the other beds before returning his vision to Steele. By comparison he looked sprightly. 'How you doing?' he asked, instantly realising how stupid it sounded. It was what you did though when confronted with the unexpected.

'Better than this lot,' Steele scanned the room, his eyes settling on a body opposite, nearest the window. 'He's had the bedpan twice this morning, think it's not long before it's the last rites. Bloody depressing. I need to get out.'

'Have they said you could...'

'I need you to nip back to mine and get me some clothes, the ones I was wearing are ruined.' he instructed, then, 'If you don't mind. I'll recover better at home, at least there the only shite I'll smell is my own.'

Mansell smirked. 'Mmm, 'tis rather pungent right enough. There's been another murder.' He added with a sigh, unsure how Steele would take it.

Steele sat down on the bed. 'From your expression I'm not going to like this.'

'Bob McLean,' Mansell said quietly. 'Beaten about the head in his own flat.'

Steele stared at the tiled floor and shook his head. 'Fuck sake!' he whispered. 'You think it's connected to the McBride case?'

'Probably,' Mansell started. 'but there was one thing.' He paused for a second. 'The fingers on his right hand had been hacked at, in the same manner her tongue was.'

'Poor sod,' Steele stood upright and gathered his things. 'Definitely no point in hanging about here a second longer.'

'You've no idea who "Haud it" and "Daud it" have lifted for it though,' added Mansell. 'That might put a smile on your face.'

'Who?'

'Harry Spencer,' Mansell laughed.

'Couple of fannies! Jesus! One night off and the place falls apart. Any chance of giving me a lift home to get changed?"

'Not a bother,' answered Mansell. 'sooner you're out of here the better.'

24

He carefully placed the phone back in its holder, didn't want to slam it down and let the hoi polloi know that he was upset about something, didn't want them knowing anything at all about him. That was the way he had got on, that was his path to success, tell them less than they needed to know and hold something, something vital, back for yourself. Inside he was volcanic though. Charlotte and the boys weren't coming back, not even to pick up their stuff. It was all in the hands of lawyers now, lawyers and her family. Her fucking family, fucking blood's thicker than water family. Wankers the lot of them. He'd tried to get on with them, but they were just common wankers at the end of the day. There was no point in pretending. No "wank, wank, good guy" like in the sketch show, just "wank, wank, wank, wank, and yet another, "wank"!

He knew that one of the ants he worked alongside would sooner or later find out about him and Charlotte, she had worked there until two years ago and still kept in touch with some of the girls in the arrears department, but they wouldn't hear it from him, they wouldn't hear him snivel or see any sign of weakness or defeat from him. He was good at hiding his emotions, he'd done it most of his life, after all. Ever since he'd been sent to The Village aged four.

He stood up to his full height and locked his PC before pushing his chair under the desk. He stretched and cracked his back before walking silently past the drones, not catching any of their eyes. Out in the corridor he thought about waiting for the lift, but thought better of it and took the stairs two at a time. Outside the rain had abated but he still pulled his thigh length coat around him, the wind was howling. He passed some tourists photographing The Abbey on his right-hand side and tutted internally. Some roadies were unloading equipment for a tribute band as he passed The Town Hall. He felt like doing more than tutting, he was on the point of shouting insanely at them. The Quintessential Queen, they were called. Why did they not just call themselves "We're Pissing On Freddie's Grave" and be done with it. Bastards! He rounded to the left and across the bridge. He passed the war memorial headed to County Square. He entered The Last Post, former post office turned massive pub, and headed straight for the toilets. Inside he found a cubicle, checked the seat was clean and sat down. He punched the door hard with his right fist. He punched it again before bawling his eyes out. Now he had no one

25

It was late in the day, but Steele needed to see Bob McLean's beaten body. He was sure he wouldn't gauge any further clues from it – Mansell had been thorough in his summation – he just needed to see it for himself. Bob McLean was him. Him in a different profession, him by a different twist of gene pool fate.

The guy who had let him into the mortuary was new to him, Steele was sure he wasn't new to the job though – he was as happy as a sandboy to let him in. "We're open twenty-four hours – death never sleeps!" he had remarked chirpily. He had then left Steele alone with the cadaver that once housed an inquisitive, talented and unscrupulous reporter.

Steele stared at the square piece of white linen that had been placed on Bob McLean's nether regions. A quick waft of wind would leave him completely naked on his stainless steel trolley. McLean's body resembled a model from a Lucien Freud painting in size and form – bloated and blotchy from years of self-abuse. It was not the body of a man who got the chance to show it off very often, either at a gymnasium or in the throes of romance. He wondered if McLean had ever had someone – a sweetheart to make his diseased heart beat faster. He had never talked of anyone, never had the time. Steele frowned, it was like they were living parallel lives. The last time he had had anyone and anything of note in his love life had been over five years ago now. He shook the thought from his head and he picked up McLean's right hand, the blood on the three fingers that had been severed now black and encrusted. 'Why?' he thought. He placed the hand of Bob McLean back on the stainless steel with care. He had seen countless corpses, and that's all they were – vessels that had stopped working for one reason or another. This was different, it felt different, more personal than the rest. Too close to home. He had only seen him on Sunday for Christ's sake! He had been full of life, ebullient, another sniff of a story in his nostrils had shot him back to life from the sorry slumber that was being a reporter in Paisley. He felt he was on to something big and it had invigorated him, breathed life into his overused lungs. And now here he was dead on a stainless steel trolley with just a piece of cloth the size of a flannel protecting whatever dignity he once had. Robert Steele wiped a tear from his eye and his fingers gently touched the forehead of the reporter. 'See you Bob, I'll miss you.'

He left the mortuary and headed for the nearest pub, The Crown. His first words were not to order a drink, but to ask if they had a cigarette machine.

26

Harry Spencer had been here before, the last time he had an egg roll for breakfast, scrambled. This time it was a cup of stewed tea with, no doubt, some spit in it. He left it untouched as he sat on his bunk. They never detained him when he had actually broken the law, but now that he was as innocent as a baby they were handcuffing him to the bed. Jesus! He really had had enough. Murder? Never in a million years. Sure, there had been people in his life deserving of being despatched, but he didn't have it in his heart to tut loudly at them never mind see them off into the great blue yonder.

Sure, he knew the lawyer, but had actually been a bit remorseful when he had heard about her murder, but this old reporter they were talking about – he'd never heard of him. When he had been marched to the desk he had asked to see Steele, at least he had always been straight with him, never tried to stitch him up.

The two detectives who had come to his flat to arrest him had made sure they were present when the desk sergeant processed him (they had made sure they had been present, they wanted the glory!) Then they had escorted him to his cell and one of them had given him a quick punch to the kidneys when his back was turned. "The camera in here doesn't work I'm afraid, so there's no point in complaining about that." Even to Harry, he thought, they sounded like a couple of lightweight fannies. As he crumpled onto the bed, the blinding pain causing his eyes to close over, they had handcuffed his right hand to the far edge of the bed nearest the wall. This made access to the toilet completely impossible. He had wet himself at two in the morning. He had no idea what time it was now, but he was soaked and stinking and needing to pee again.

He heard the door rattle and open and there they were again, the two idiots.

'Jesus! Said McGlaughlin. 'You dirty wee...' he never finished, simply grabbed his nostrils.

'I couldn't reach the toilet,' Spencer started. 'You had handcuffed me to the...'

Slap. Patterson caught him across the face. 'Enough with your excuses.' He reached across and undid the cuff on Harry Spencer's right wrist.

Harry Spencer instinctively grabbed at his released wrist and rubbed it.

His movement surprised Patterson, causing him to slap Spencer again. Through the open door WPC Mhairi MacKay witnessed the second slap.

She coughed to let Patterson know that she was there, but he simply turned and waved for McGlaughlin to close the door over. 'Mind your own business love.' He snapped. 'Man's work,' he smirked at his companion.

'I'm bursting for a pee,' Spencer bleated, close to tears, his red eyes unable to catch Patterson's.

'What you waiting on then?' McGlaughlin asked him. 'An invitation.'

He stood and waddled towards the toilet, undid his soaking denims and pulled them and his boxers down around his thighs. He sighed audibly as he let go. He heard them whisper behind him. 'We can't take him in for interview stinking like that.' Patterson muttered. 'That's your fault for cuffing him there.'

'How was I to know he was going to...'

'If we get him a shower they'll ask questions and we'll get bollocked at the very least.'

'If anybody asks we'll just deny he was cuffed.' McGlaughlin started. 'Tell them that pishing himself was one of his protests.'

'Good idea,' Patterson acquiesced. 'He is well known for them after all.' The two sniggered like complicit bullies. Their voices were now at a level where Spencer could hear every word without straining to be heard over the noise of his urine hitting the stainless steel of the toilet. He finished and as he was pulling up his soaking trousers he heard McGlaughlin suggest with a laugh, 'Bad cop, bad cop?'

'Couple of dicks!'

'What did you call us?' McGlaughlin roared at Spencer.

'It wasn't him, it was me.'

Patterson and McGlaughlin turned and saw the figure of Rob Steele standing in the now open doorway. He was flanked by Mansell and WPC Mhairi McKay.

'Is this your "man's work" is it?' Steele asked. 'I'd suggest you two retire to your desks and think of a good excuse as to why Bain shouldn't chain you to them for the rest of what's left of your careers.'

As The Two Johns passed Mhairi McKay McGlaughlin hissed 'Grass.' She made no reply.

Steele looked at the figure of Harry Spencer in front of him and shook his head. 'Let's get you a shower son.'

27

As Blair Devine drove past Reid Kerr college he smiled. Last night had been the third good night's sleep in a row and he had considered doing without his anti-depressant, but Belinda had left them on the breakfast bar for him like some benevolent carer before going to her coffee morning at the golf club. He had slept until nine. Nine! It was unheard of. He had no appointments until half one so had decided to indulge himself. He had tried in the shower, but he couldn't maintain his focus, or erection for that matter. No matter how much he had in the boot of his car there was nothing better than the thrill of the chase, the seeking out of new quarry. He fancied a pair of high heels.

But where? Where in paisley at this time of the day – it was now ten thirty-five according to the clock on the dash. Nowhere, that's where. Paisley wasn't awash with divas. Junkies, whores and backstabbers yes, but divas? They were to be found elsewhere, somewhere a bit more upbeat, where the people had more to live for. Silverburn, that's where he'd find an office administrator, or credit controller with a day off work and a yearning for shoe shopping. Women always got dolled up to go shopping, especially for shoes.

He took the left by the abandoned bowling alley and stopped at the traffic lights on the junction of Glasgow Road and Mill Street. As he waited he gazed at the entrance to the police station, fully expecting to see Harry Spencer being released, thus throwing him into a new pit of depression. He saw nothing of the kind and carried on past the tannery (the stench was often weak at this time of the day) and turned left onto the Barrhead Road. As he went by the tin houses at Hunterhill he remembered a former learner – couldn't recall her name – but she had attempted to wear high heels on her first lesson. He remembered that as he sent her back in to change her footwear, the clacking of the heels on her path had caused him to stiffen and he had nearly knocked one out there and then. Of course, he was a professional, he had waited until the lesson was finished and found a quiet spot in the Morrisons' car park to relieve himself.

He turned left at The Hurlet and in no time was seeking out a spot in the Silverburn car park as close to the entrance as he could find without stealing into a disabled spot. He eventually found one between two black 4x4s. He sat for a while, judging the distance he would have to run should the worst case scenario raise its' ugly head. He had run from security guards before, but that was many years ago. The last time he had attempted a snatch from a shop he was in his late twenties. Jesus, where did the time go? He scratched at his bald pate and plucked a hair from his ear. Firstly, he'd have to get by the shop security, that's if he was spotted. Then there was always someone lurking by the main exits. What the hell was he thinking? There was no way on God's green earth he'd get away with this. He slapped his hairless head. 'Get a grip Blair, get a grip!' That was just it, he needed to get a grip. Of himself, of his flaccid tool. It was only the shoes that satisfied him now, the thought of a bare foot sweating inside them. He needed a fresh one though, the ones he had accumulated in the boot had long since lost their odour and allure. They had taken on the aroma of the boot of a car. Hardly sexy. Beggars couldn't be choosers though, so he pressed the boot unlock button on the dash and opened his door. As he opened the boot he glanced into the back of the 4x4 to his right. On the back seat there sat a discarded pair of blue shoes, heels four inches high. He felt his groin twitch nervously, and in a matter of seconds, without even touching himself he was fully erect. He couldn't help himself, this moment was too good to waste. While his left hand was holding up the boot of the car (it afforded him a degree of privacy, just a degree), his right was plunged down his brown corduroys and had started to get busy. He couldn't take his eyes off the shoes, imagining the alabaster feet inside them, delicate size fives, he imagined, painted toe nails – red he hoped.

'Hey you ya dirty bas...'

Blair looked to his right, his hand instinctively coming out of his trousers. He saw a car park attendant running toward him, waving a fist He was paralysed, feeling his cock stiffen then sink like the Bismarck, a trail of hot slime sticking to the inside of his speedo briefs. He wanted so much to have completed his mission with all hands-on deck, but he had sunk like a stone after abandoning ship. He felt no pleasure, just sticky, just disgusting. He felt his flaccid member twitch for the last time before the attendant had a hand on his shoulder.

'Ya dirty beggar...'

28

Steele was now regretting a decision he had made first thing. He had woken disgusted with himself for being so weak as to purchase another packet of cigarettes. He had paid a king's ransom for them and yet had smoked only six. The rest he threw in his bin as soon as he was showered and dressed. A new day a new start. But now he was sitting opposite DCI Bain wishing he was smoking his head off.

'We don't appear to be any further along Robert,' he shook his head sanctimoniously. 'It's been since Sunday; the trail will be cold.'

'Mmm,' the slow drag of a high tar fag, how magnificent.

'And the chief suspect in the Gallowhill murder is still on the lam,' he sighed.

"On the lam!" thought Steele, what was this? Gangbusters? 'To be fair sir,' Steele started. 'I have been in hospital. I'm not using it as an excuse, but it's eaten into the time we've had.' Lighting a second cigarette from the glowing embers of the one you've nearly finished.

'So what do we have?'

'Well,' Steele slouched in the chair. 'Uniform is on the lookout for Garry McCulloch, prime suspect in the murder of Rachel Boyd from Gallowhill,' Steele enjoyed watching Bain squirm as he named the Gallowhill victim. 'McBride and McLean I think are linked, but at this point we're cold as to why. McBride was involved in a divorce with Garry McCulloch's cousin, Alisdair. Also, she was involved in a case with Harry Spencer, who we currently have in custody. McLean was involved with him as well – couple of dodgy headlines that made him a laughing stock, but my heart tells me he's not our man...'

'How can you be so certain?' boomed Bain. 'Everything points to him.'

'It's not him,' Steele said calmly. 'You have to trust me on this, it's instinct.'

'When did instinct ever solve a crime?' Bain's bald head shook nervously, his face reddening. 'Robert, I want results, not excuses.'

'Even if it's the wrong result?' Steele snapped back. 'McBride was also involved in some sort of swingers' club in the west end,' he paused and let Bain take that one in. 'A club frequented by our old friend Maurice Sanderson.' He again paused and could see Bain shrinking into his seat at the thought of Sanderson and McBride together. 'Also a visitor to this establishment was a certain Alisdair McCulloch, and his wife...' Steele couldn't recall the name.

'Jean,' Bain reminded him.

Steele paused before talking again and gave Bain a look. A look suggesting that he too was involved in some way.

'Don't be ridiculous Steele!' he blurted. 'There's no way I'd be involved in any shenanigans of that nature.'

'Just thought I'd put it out there sir,' Steele laughed. 'Everybody else seems to be involved in it.'

'What about the husband?' Bain asked. 'Of the braes murder?' Bain let that one linger with Steele, two could play his game.

'Very good sir,' Steele mused. 'A strange one. He is now, as far as I'm aware, one of the only openly gay golfers in...' he wasn't sure how far to cast his net. 'In Paisley at least.'

'Really?' Bain was astonished, there was certainly no one at his club of "that" persuasion.

'He's the pro at The Paisley Golf Club, in the Braes, don't know if we'd glean anything from another chat, but we'll see.'

Bain's ears pricked up at the mention of where McBride worked. 'He would know the area.'

'He's got an alibi.' Steele countered.

'That must count for something,' Bain clearly wasn't listening.

'He's got an alibi.' Christ, he needed a cigarette.

'Yes,' Bain cleared his throat. 'But these people and their lifestyle, it's...'

'Alibi,' Steele had had enough and was grateful that the phone rang and almost drowned out his one word retort.

Bain answered it and listened for a couple of seconds before covering the mouthpiece and speaking. 'Thanks Robert, keep me in the loop.'

"In the loop?" Steele mused as he closed the door behind him. If anyone in the building was less "in the loop" than Bain, he had yet to meet him. The man was a dinosaur, old school "clip round the ear" policing.

Back at his office Steele found Mansell talking to a cleaned up Harry Spencer. He had kitted him out in clothes from the lost and found. He had on a pair of ladies' brush velvet pink sweat pants and a St Mirren strip that was at least four sizes too big for him.

'Looking good son,' Steele quipped. I'd be okay wearing the trousers, but I'd draw the line at a bloody St Mirren top.' He turned his attention to Mansell. 'Have you no shame?'

'He picked them boss,' Mansell shrugged. 'Now what are we going to do with you Mr Spencer? You keep turning up like some bad penny.'

'It's not my fault. I've been trying not to get into bother, it was that other two that lifted me,' he pleaded. 'All I want is a bit of custody to the Wee Man.'

Dykebar? Thought Mansell, that's what this one needed, some serious therapy, heavy duty deep cleaning. 'You have to stop thinking about it Harry,' he said solemnly. 'He's not your boy. It's not your fight and the more high profile you are in the community - what with your protests and everything – the more idiots like Patterson and McGlaughlin are going to put two and two together and get five. You're a prime candidate for lifting. If you didn't do it, they'll pin it on you anyway.'

Steele coughed loudly at this suggestion. 'Of course, corruption on that scale is extremely rare in this police station. Everything by the book and if you veer off that line the book in question gets thrown at you.' Christ, thought Steele, he had nearly convinced himself. He fished into his pocket and pulled out two twenties and pushed them across the desk to Spencer. 'Take that to get your clothes cleaned up. Don't worry about returning the ones you've got on, just have a look at them every time you think you're about to do something stupid.'

Spencer was confused, but his hand edged towards the money. 'Is this a bribe?' he asked. 'To buy my silence? They two beat me up you know, I should press charges.'

Steele shook his head slowly and sighed. 'It's not a bribe son, just take it. And don't you worry about those two tubes, they'll get theirs. Just take it.'

He took it and placed it in the pocket of his pink sweat pants. They felt really comfortable, he might wear them round the house.

'Let's get you out of here,' Steele stood up. 'I'll see you out, make sure you're at least off police property before you do yet another daft thing.'

'Don't worry Mr Steele,' Spencer told him. 'I'll keep my nose clean.'

As Spencer and Steele passed the booking in desk on the way to the exit Blair Devine was getting processed. They heard the words "public indecency in a carpark" and not much else. Devine caught Spencer's eye and looked terrified. They were releasing him; they were releasing him for God's sake! 'Don't let him go!' he hollered. 'He's a murderer!'

It wasn't until Spencer and Steele were the other side of the glass door that Harry Spencer recognised his former driving instructor. He looked so dishevelled, had less hair than before as well. He waved in a friendly manner towards Blair Devine, who all of a sudden looked at Harry Spencer in a terrified manner. 'Wonder what his problem is?' he said to Steele as they got outside.

'You just worry about yourself son,' Steele suggested. 'Let other people deal with their own shit.' He patted Spencer on the back. 'Remember, straight home, and we don't want to see you again.'

He watched him walk off. He cut a hilarious sight in women's trousers and a shirt that doubled up as a kaftan. 'God help you.'

Harry Spencer went straight home, got changed, phoned his brother and within an hour was steaming. The two twenty pound notes soon disappeared.

29

It was the way he had looked at him that sent a chill down his spine. Those eyes, so cold, like he didn't care, like Blair didn't know he was coming for him next. By God he was good. So nonchalant, in the bloody police station as well! Blair Devine had spent a fitful night in a holding cell – not due to the prospect of ending up in jail permanently and banished to the sex offenders register and all the penury that brought with it. No doubt Belinda would leave him, now there was a silver lining, knowing his luck she'd stay and torment him every day about what he had done. He doubted he would notice the difference. No, the beatings in jail for being a nonce or the slavering acceptance of other weirdos he would no doubt end up mixing with held no fear for him. It was Spencer. Harry Spencer. The man must have blood of ice. He didn't care about daily beatings or being touched up by perverts for the rest of his life, he just didn't want to die. His life might have been a pitiful reflection of other peoples, but it was his life, and the thought of being on Spencer's hit list chilled him. He was a breathing sentient being with no desire to be tortured and hacked to death by a student he had let slip through his net.

The night in the cell had done him the world of good. He thought it through and decided to take the bull by the horns and other such metaphors. If the mountain was slowly creeping up on Mohammed, then he decided it was time Big Mo clipped on his crampons and took to the hills. He located the house phone down the side of the settee and checked his battered red book for the number. It rang out without going to an answer phone. He tapped the phone against his head for a few seconds before pressing redial. It rang twice before being answered.

'Hullo,' the voice was gruff and sleepy.

'Hello,' Blair's voice was chipper and upbeat, he had the bull firmly in his grasp. 'Is that you Harry?' Friendly and pleasant without any hint of guilt.

'Aye,' Blair Devine could almost picture the confused expression on Harry Spencer's face.

'It's Blair, Blair Devine, BDSM?' he let it hang for a while. 'Listen Harry, I was looking through the books the other night and your name came up, so I thought I'd give you a call.'

Spencer interrupted, seemingly sure in which direction the conversation was headed. 'You listen Blair, I don't have any money, I paid you for every less...'

'Stop, stop, stop, stop, stop.' Blair Devine laughed out loud, it was a fake laugh, but only he knew that. 'You've got the wrong end of the stick Harry, let me finish. So, I'd a look through the accounts, well, in truth it was my wife, you know me and my head for figures?' he didn't wait on a reply just charged on. 'Anyhoo, Belinda found that you had paid for a whole block booking that you hadn't taken, the introductory offer, pay for ten lessons get ten free? You remember?' Of course you don't remember, it's bollocks! Everything's bollocks. 'So, you're owed ten lessons, and I was thinking after seven we could apply for your test, because you were so close last time Harry, it'd be a shame to waste your chance. What do you say?'

Harry Spencer said nothing, wondering if he was still dreaming. Something for nothing? Surely not, where was the catch? 'How much is it going to cost me? Cause I don't have a bean.'

'Nothing, nada, zilch.' Yet another fake laugh. 'Ten free lessons you've paid for them already. It was an accounts glitch.'

'But I don't remember a buy ten get ten free offer,' Spencer was doing his best to talk himself out of it.

'To tell you the truth Harry neither do I,' God he was convincing. 'It was my wife, if it was down to me I wouldn't have phoned you, but she's got such a sense of justice and fair play.' Sure she has. 'So? You up for your first lesson today, an hour's time? You still living at the same address?'

'Eh, aye...'

'Great!' Blair Devine suddenly felt a change of career coming on – acting. 'Pick you up in an hour then.' He switched the phone off. He would be out of pocket, but he would be alive. Spencer would spare him, strike him off his list. It was genius, absolute genius.

30

'What is it again?' Steele threw the statement into the air at Mansell. 'Born on a Sunday, buried on a Saturday, that Solomon Grundy thing?'

'Well,' Mansell began. 'I know it's not murdered on a Sunday and...' Steele's look halted him in his tracks.

'Bit of respect son,' he smiled. 'Bit of respect. Hello!' Steele and Mansell had been at the church service for Georgina McBride. They had sat at the very back there, and now at the graveside they were stood a good fifty yards and a sea of monumental masonry away from the burial site. It had been family, friends and colleagues and the minister had spoken of her warmly – like he actually knew her. At this point Steele and Mansell had shared a schoolboy look, wondering if he was in any way involved in The Renfrewshire Rope and Twine Co. They had to physically stop themselves from sniggering and getting thrown out. Grief brings out different emotions in people, but childish hilarity was very rarely quoted as one of them. The only "face" of note had been Maurice Sanderson, pressing the flesh with everyone he could after the service. He was so sincere as he approached John, her widower and his lover. The man was a consummate sleaze, Steele had decided. If he possibly had anything to do with Georgina's death, then he was hiding it remarkably well.

'Seen him boss,' Mansell replied. 'The usual couple of heavies with him as well.'

'No show without somebody that can punch, eh?' Steele was pleased with himself, but Mansell simply glowered at him.

'Cracker,' he sighed.

The two men were staring intently at the sight of Alisdair McCulloch and a couple of his henchmen clambering out of a shining black SUV, parked a short distance from the main action at the graveside. Steele peered and saw the gangster's body was visibly stooped as though racked by grief. He was wrong, Alisdair McCulloch had noticed his shoelace was loose and bent down to tie it. He then raised himself to his full height – six two in his stocking soles – and strode towards the graveside, single red rose in hand, ushering his henchmen to stay behind. The burial rites had been completed, and all that was left was for those mourners who wanted to throw earth or flowers on top of the coffin to do so. McCulloch cut through the gathered crowd virtually unseen by the rest of the mourners. All but Sanderson, who nodded to him as he passed nearby. At the graveside, McCulloch kissed the rose and dropped it into the hole in the ground. He then, again, cut through the crowd unnoticed and made his way back to the car. Sanderson watched him all the way. As did Mansell and Steele.

'Think it's time we paid uncle Alisdair a visit,' Steele nodded to Mansell. 'Let's get to the car and follow him. It's amazing the information you can glean from a funeral.'

'The Shireen's not so bad either,' Mansell nodded towards some of McBride's colleagues, festooned in the funereal black. 'There's just something about the funeral uniform that does it for me.'

'Death and sex, that's all there is.' Steele said as they made for the car. 'And taxes.'

'Okay Freud,' Mansell took the keys from his jacket pocket. 'I hope he's not going far, I've not got much petrol.'

They weren't going far, from the crematorium at Woodside, down Broomlands Street before turning left onto the one-way system, turning left just before the railway bridge at Incle Street. They went along the side of the railway for thirty yards on a dirt track road and got to their destination. Junction 47, one of, if not, *the*, grottiest pub in Paisley. And that was saying something.

'With all his money,' Steele sighed. 'He chooses this place?'

'You can take the scumbag out the scheme, but not the scheme out the scumbag,' Mansell chirruped.

'Quite,' Steele agreed. 'Hang back a bit, don't want to get clocked.'

Mansell's lips pursed together, he had been doing that since they had come out from behind the tree! 'Whatever you say,' he whispered sarcastically, drawing a look from his superior. 'Have we got a plan?'

Steele exhaled, 'I suppose a plan would be good,' he scratched at the lobe of his right ear. 'We'll see how it goes.'

'What about back up?'

'Back up would be good as well, I suppose,' Steele grimaced. 'That would involve a lot of questions from our beloved leader, and I'm not sure I've got all the answers to them at present. Let's just wing it.'

Mansell shook his head, 'Well, I'm reassured to know that we're not going in half cocked, as it were.'

They made their way from the car, across the gravel forecourt and Steele's hand gripped the handle of the door to the pub and pulled when he should have pushed.

31

Harry Spencer was stood at his window trying to look casual. It had to be a joke. Trying to convince an on looking world that he had something better to do than to stand at the window and wait for his first driving lesson in over six months. A free driving lesson! He had seen people like it, relaxed people, in life and movies, and wanted to be like them. Put the lesson to the back of his mind until the very last minute (if indeed it ever happened), until Blair turned into the street and tooted his horn. Until then he could be reading an important novel, putting up a shelf, seeing to that leaky tap, writing witty emails to interesting friends in far flung lands. But when he heard the toot of the horn he would drop everything and head out to the car. He wasn't like that though, his life was no movie, if it was the word "disaster" appeared in front of it, of that he was certain. He eyed the clock on the wall, five minutes until the official kick off, realising there wasn't any point in him looking out anyway. Blair had only ever been on time once, for his first lesson. The rest of the time he had started every lesson late and ended early. Initially Harry had been a bit put out by this (though God forbid he would actually say anything!) but as the lessons took on the form of torture more than they did education, he didn't mind the late starts and early finishes. He sighed and headed into the kitchen to get a drink of water to ease his dry throat. TOOT TOOT! From outside the front window as he turned the tap. He drank the water in one go and placed the glass rim down on the drainer without washing it – there was only him now, nothing to catch there. He returned to the living room and saw that it was Blair's black Astra parked on the other side of the road. Blair stood on the pavement on the passenger's side of the car, his balding head looking red and sore in the brilliant sunlight. It had been chucking it down until five minutes ago, and now as his lesson dawned the sun had charged through dark clouds to smile on the streets. He waved and smiled at Harry, beckoning him down. It had to be a joke, thought Harry. He'd get in the driver's seat, start the ignition and suddenly find himself staring down at the laughing Blair as the ejector seat sent him soaring towards the sun. Ha ha clunk, he'd laugh his head off at that.

No joke. He turned the ignition, gear in neutral and hand brake on, his clown-like imagination waiting for the big whoosh, but nothing untoward happened.

'Good Harry,' Blair nervously fastened his seat belt. 'Now what are you going to do next?' He rubbed his sweaty palms together, staring at the side of the killers' head. He didn't have the eyes of a killer, but then again, these days everyone seemed capable of being culpable. Just look at any newspaper.

'Indicate and pull off,' answered Harry.

'And?'

'And get up to speed with all the other traffic on the road.' He answered confidently.

'No,' Blair found it hard not to bark at his students these days, but he would have to make an exception here. 'I mean, before you indicate?' He wanted to scream MIRROR! SIGNAL! MANOEUVRE! but stopped himself. 'It was the first thing I told you to do.

'Oh right.'

Blair watched awestruck as Hapless Harry wrestled with the seat and pushed it back. 'No!' he screeched, then caught himself and spoke quietly. 'Mirror, signal, manoeuvre. Remember? You've got to check behind yourself. Your blind spot?'

'Right, right right,' Harry sat upright although the chair wasn't quite right now.

'So?' Blair said softly.

'No problem.' Harry put the car in gear and took off without looking, straight into the path of an oncoming black transit. 'Whoops,' he smiled, seeing the driver of the van apoplectic in the rear view mirror.

Blair panicked, not wanting to force Harry's hand, thus speeding his own demise. 'That was a bit hasty Harry,' he placated the deadly student. 'You've got up to second fine, but what about third?'

Harry pointed at the road ahead, the car veering towards those parked on his left hand-side. Blair grabbed the wheel and straightened it up. 'Cheers,' he said nonchalantly. 'There's a junction ahead and I'll have to go back down to at least second anyway.'

'That's about fifty metres away!' Blair yelped. 'But you're probably right, no point in troubling the engine for a mere fifty metres.'

Harry chugged the car until it was ten metres from the junction. He kept pressing at the accelerator gingerly until the car finally came to a halt just before the line.

'Bit slow on the approach,' Blair was doing his best to remain constructive. 'You want to go left, so get the indicator on nice and early.'

He watched in horror as Harry indicated right. He leant over and adjusted the control. 'Easy mistake to make.'

Realising the car was almost stopped Harry stuck his foot down heavily on the accelerator. The car lurched forward across the give way lines and into the middle of the junction. Two cars, both Skoda taxis, screeched to a halt inches from Blair's paintwork. The sound of their horns was deafening, and Blair held up an apologetic hand to both drivers.

'Sorry about that,' Harry grimaced.

'Maybe let me take over for a second,' Blair suggested. 'Rest your feet and I'll reverse us up.' His heart was trying to tear out of his chest as he swirled the steering wheel with one hand and navigated his car back towards the give way lines. The two mini cab drivers scowled, swore and gestured towards him as they made their way left and right. Nagged in stereo. 'Right Harry. Do not turn or pull out until I tell you. What the f...' Blair turned and saw that the driver of the transit they had initially pulled out in front of was opening the passenger side door. 'What do you think yo...' He felt a large fist crack the side of his head and fell on to the gear stick.

32

The inside of Junction 47 reeked of body odour and desperation. Through the patchy gloom it was possible only to make out the whites of eyes and the vague shapes of drinkers slumped over the beers on their tables. Steele and Mansell gave their eyes a few seconds to adjust to the half light before moving any farther forward. As they did so the doors to the toilet – the other side of the bar – swung like someone was needing to use the facilities in a great hurry. The inconsistent clumps of gloom were an easy hiding place for any potential attacker. 'Bit like being at the pictures,' Steele whispered to Mansell.

'Mmm,' Mansell wasn't happy and wanted to turn right back around again. McCulloch was dangerous, especially on his own turf. Junction 47 was a lawless hovel within which their jurisdiction counted for very little. They would have to bring their "A" game into play if they were to get out of here in one piece. He was about to voice his concerns to Steele when the DI stepped forward and immersed himself in the gloom. He began walking towards a table to the left of the bar, nearest the toilets. Mansell followed behind like a reluctant puppy, out of step with his superior, he looked awkward trying to catch up.

'Well, well, well,' Steele almost laughed, it sounded too much like Hello hello hello. 'Alisdair McCulloch as I live and choke.' He peered at the corner table where the hood was holding court with a couple of his heavies

McCulloch recognised the baritone voice. 'Rob Steele,' he cackled back. 'The most inappropriately named policeman on the planet.' He didn't want to say anything further, let Steele do the chasing.

Steele crossed the floor focussed on the figure in the corner, Mansell followed on his coattails, checking out the eyes that traced their path, eyes so sunken you'd need a shovel and a map to dig them up. He looked to the right at the barman, fists on the bar, no respecter of outside justice. It wasn't just the alcohol in the bar that was poisonous, Mansell thought, there was real venom hovering just above the surface, about to boil over. He knew better than to open his mouth without Steele doing so first. He had summed up the contents of the bar and didn't fancy their chances should the venom be released. He didn't fancy ending up buried under some railway sleeper in the middle of nowhere, and in this bar that felt like a very real possibility.

Steele was within feet of the table when McCulloch next spoke. 'Must be important for you to come here Mr Steele. Thought you knew this place was out of bounds to your lot.'

Steele pulled a chair towards himself, scraping the feet on the lino. 'I know that Mr McCulloch, but you must know boundaries are there to be crossed, rules there to be broken.'

McCulloch scowled at the small talk and threw back a rum and coke. 'Get to the point, then get out.' He took a look at Mansell. 'Cause I don't fancy you and your boy's chances when push comes to shove, when rules are there to be broken. Billy,' he held his empty glass in the air. 'Another.'

'Not for us thanks,' Steele shouted to the sullen barman. 'Crimes to solve, bad guys to catch, you know how it is?' He returned his focus to McCulloch. 'I want, sorry, I'll start that again, give you the respect you deserve. I'd quite like to talk to you Mr McCulloch with or without that dick cousin of yours who, it would appear, is hiding in the toilet. No doubt shitting himself, even though his relation is the maddest, baddest ne'er-do-well in the parish.' Steele had taken a punt on the swinging door, and from the bile pouring from McCulloch's eyes he could see that it had paid off. 'Actually, you might want to let him stew in there, cause I'm not sure his wee sensitive ears should hear what we want to talk to you about.'

'Ach get to the point Steele,' McCulloch growled.

'Georgina McBride?' Steele left it hanging but saw the malice in the maddest, baddest ne'er-do-well's eyes had been replaced by something akin to tears. 'I've been hearing stories about you and your, soon to be, ex-wife and a certain swingers club and when I go to investigate, here, don't I find out that she's the lawyer representing your, soon to be...'

'Enough Steele,' McCulloch growled quietly and menacingly. 'For a kick off – let's get this straight, I had nothing to do with that lassie's murder. If I find out who did, they're dead. Next, my marital strife is none of your fucking business. Jeanie and me are getting a divorce, big deal. Look at the statistics, happens all the time. As for my idiot cousin,' he eyed the toilet door. 'I'll deal with him. You lot have tried and failed.'

'Correction,' Steele moved his face in closer to McCulloch's. 'We never failed, he bolted like the shitebag he is. If he had any balls he'd have stayed and faced the music. Murder is murder, he'll have to pay.' He pointed an angry finger inches from McCulloch's nose. 'He never broke the law in here, in this hovel. He broke the law outside on my patch. I'm claiming him for the guys with the white hats and chargers.' Steele saw that his index finger was shaking, far from being with rage, it was with his own physical frailty. He prayed McCulloch didn't spot it and pulled it away from his face and sat back in his chair.

'You think I'm just going to let you take him away, just like that?' A smile appeared on McCulloch's lips. 'No chance,' he parroted, pulling a revolver from the pocket of his Barbour jacket. 'No fucking danger.'

'Mr McCulloch,' it was Mansell who was speaking, and Steele's eyes snuck a sideways look at him. He had never looked more relaxed. 'You honestly don't think that we would dare to come here empty handed, do you?'

Steele was sure he could see a smirk on Mansell's lips. What the hell was he thinking of? Had he not seen the gun?

'Billy,' McCulloch waved at the barman who was approaching with his drink. 'Check outside and see if there's any...'

'You'll not find anything Billy,' Mansell interrupted. 'Save your shoe leather. If Mill Street don't hear from us in five minutes there'll be more blue and white here than at Ibrox on a Saturday afternoon. So, I would advise you...'

'Shut up!' McCulloch lifted the gun from table level and pressed it against Mansell's well-shaven chin. 'Do you believe him?' McCulloch asked Steele rhetorically. 'Just out of nappies and he's "advising me"? Listen son, you advise me of fuck all. This gun is the only thing dishing out advice at the minute, and it advises you to make a phone call to your fat desk sergeant or whoever the hell it is you've to phone and tell them everything is fine, nothing to report. Got it?'

Mansell started laughing. As he did so Steele was sure he was about to soil himself.

'What's so funny smart boy?' asked McCulloch.

'You,' Mansell chuckled. Beside him, Steele was sure he was touching cloth. 'Do you honestly think that I'm going to make a phone call that will sign my death certificate? If you were going to shoot me you'd have done it by now, but something tells me you wouldn't want to bring that sort of trouble to your own doorstep.' Mansell looked behind him towards the door, where the barman was shaking his head to McCulloch after looking for police cars outside. 'So, if you want me to make a phone call, I can, but do you not think that we've got special coded words we can mention if we're in trouble? For example...'

'For example!' In one seamless move McCulloch turned the gun in his hand, pulled it back and cracked Mansell across the temple with it. His lifeless body whacked against Steele's shaking shoulder. Steele grabbed at his limp form as he fell. He watched as the cut on the side of Mansell's head opened and began to run with sticky blood. 'Steele!' McCulloch waved the weapon in front of the shocked D.I. 'Don't suppose there's any point in asking you to make a phone call?'

Steele didn't answer, his eyes dropped towards the bleeding head of his colleague once more. Mansell was spluttering, coming groggily back from the brink. Steele was amazed at Mansell's courage, at his ability to remain calm and gracefully eloquent under such pressure. What was all that old pony about code words though? That was straight out the Famous Five manual for foxing a villain.

'Don't you try anything stupid,' McCulloch tapped Steele's forehead with the gun. 'Garry! Get your junky arse out here. We've work to do.'

Steele noticed that the rest of the shadows who had been drinking in the bar were hastily making their way to the exit, peering out at the daylight like vampires, leaving their half finished drinks behind them. They had obviously known that "work" was some sort of codeword! Steele cradled Mansell's head, the blood hadn't come to much, and he was starting to blink, obviously in pain.

'What?' he lifted his head slowly, confusion tattooed across his eyes. He sat up in slow motion, his movements uncertain and his mouth gulping O's like a goldfish singing in a choir. His eyes narrowed as he saw the figure of Garry McCulloch exit the toilet. 'You were right sir,' he grimaced. 'It was him in the...' he sounded so childish, like the blow to the head had sent him back twenty years or more.

'I know son,' Steele whispered. 'Probably best if you save your breath for actually breathing. We're in deep shit here.'

'Deep shit,' Mansell repeated, laughing. 'That's funny sir. That's funny.'

'Shush,' Steele said without his lips moving.

'Why have we to shush?' Mansell was back to being an inquisitive six-year-old. 'The back-up will be here in a minute.'

'Shut him up Steele!' McCulloch shouted from the bar counter where he and his cronies were squeezing their arms and legs into white boiler suits. 'He's starting to get on my wick! There you are,' McCulloch leant over the bar and threw a thick roll of silver gaffer tape towards Garry. 'Make yourself useful and get them oven ready.'

'Oven ready?' slurred Mansell. 'What's that mean sir? What's that mean?' Mansell stopped talking. A strip of silver gaffer tape was placed across the place where the questions used to come from. He knew now what oven ready meant.

Garry McCulloch then set about taping his hands behind his back before turning his attention to Steele.

'You don't want to get tangled up in this so...' Steele too was silenced by the silver tape. His arms were then immobilised in the same manner as Mansell's had been.

'Shall I do their ankles as well?' he shouted over towards the bar.

His question was met with a shake of the head. 'They look heavy, and there's only the three of us. Do them when they're in the van.' McCulloch looked as Billy put on his leather jacket and headed towards the front door and closed it, snibbing it at the top and bottom.

'Out the back way,' he instructed. 'Just in case.'

'You ready?' McCulloch asked him. This question was met silently and Steele grimaced as he saw the overweight barman pull the flap of his leather jacket to reveal a polished wooden handle. No doubt a sawn off. There were some concrete foundations of a new build house waiting for them and he didn't have the strength, mental or physical to get him and his child-like colleague out of it. He was trying to call on reserve that he just didn't have at the moment, the years of drinking, smoking and avoiding exercise suddenly and dramatically catching up with him. He didn't fancy their chances at all, but he knew a man that did.

Beside him Mansell was attempting to wrestle his wrists free from the tape. Steele nodded for him to stop, realising that they had to buy as much time for themselves as possible. Mansell's wriggling would just hasten their doom. Garry noticed the wriggling and a sleekit smile crossed his murderous face. 'You think this is my first time?' he drawled. 'I've taped more punters than you've had hot...'

'GARRY!' Alisdair McCulloch slapped his cousin theatrically on the back of the head. 'Shut it.'

'But we're going to k...'

'Shut it anyway.' McCulloch pulled his leather jacket on and placed the gun in the pocket. 'You get the lights Billy?'

They were led through a back cellar, the concrete floor wet with spilt beer, through a fire exit and out into the back of the car park where the back doors of a white transit beckoned them.

33

After a couple of seconds of bemusement Blair sat back upright, the driver of the van was now negotiating his way round the stricken learner car. Blair watched him as he proffered a less than friendly gesture in his general direction and drove off.

'You know,' Harry Spencer muttered. 'We could follow him and we could both sort him out.'

Blair was suddenly aghast, his student's idea of "sorting people out" causing his mind's eye to be filled with torrents of blood and fresh lacerations. He shook his head. 'Don't you worry about it Harry,' he replied. 'Just one of the hazards of the job. There's always one impatient idiot out there not willing to give the learner driver a chance.' Give the learner driver a chance? Jesus! he thought. Spencer just didn't have it, not before and not now, but he had no desire to incur his wrath and end up in any way dead. So, keeping this accident waiting to happen behind the wheel sweet and up to test standard was paramount. He couldn't give up before he'd even started. 'Right.' he tried to sound as enthusiastic as he could, all the while his fingers traced the cap of the bottle of anti-depressants in his pocket. 'Maybe we should go somewhere quiet and practice some of the basic manoeuvres. Start the engine.'

Harry turned the key and the car stuttered forward, causing Blair to grab at the wheel. 'You're still in gear. Turn off the engine then foot on the clutch and into neutral.' He took the bottle of pills from his pocket and poured two into his palm.

'For your nerves?' laughed Harry.

'No no,' he lied. 'Just antibiotics for a chest infection. Nothing serious.' Far, far away, that's where he wanted to be. As far away from his present life as possible. He pondered whether an instructor had ever taken his own life in the middle of a lesson. He shook the thought and waited for the effects of his "wee happy pills" to kick in. 'Take a left here Harry and we'll head up the Neilston Road towards Potterhill. That'll be quiet this time of the day. Steady as we go, remember to give it plenty of revs before releasing the hand brake.' Most lessons he could do on auto-pilot mode, but he never could with Spencer, he was just too erratic.

34

Steele wondered if Mansell was trying to attempt anything stupid, whether he had another Famous Five plan up his tethered sleeve? He couldn't look to find out, they had been placed back to back on the floor of the van, a large sheet of blue tarpaulin stopping any of their DNA from escaping onto the actual bodywork of the vehicle. It was difficult to assess any movement beside him, the van's suspension being in such a state of disrepair that going over the slightest pebble caused cataclysmic juddering. He had tried initially to sit up, but McCulloch had not been bragging unrealistically about his ability with a roll of gaffer tape and a hostage. He felt paralysed, the only movement being his head banging occasionally on the floor as the van encountered yet more pebbles on the road. His sense of direction was screwed, at the outset he had tried to figure out with the turning of each corner in which direction they were heading, but it was all too stop/start and he gave up. He just gave up. Like he had before and now, in the pitch black of the back of a van, his mind and heart turned to the dark side.

He vividly recalled his wedding photographs. Every face in the correct order in which they stood on the day, Harry next to Betty, his mother and father next to Sheila's parents, Jimmy next to Francine, his Hallowe'en cake face booming even in the monochrome of the snaps. George next to Marion, Sadie next to Davey. And on and on, all beaming electric smiles. All except for himself and Sheila, their expressions a mix of reluctance and acceptance. The only thing missing from the photo being the shotgun looming overhead. For that's what it was. Neither of them in love, but both too decent to do the wrong thing. They went through with it for the sake of the burgeoning bump in Sheila's womb.

He remembered trying, ever so slightly, trying to make it work. He remembered waiting for her to go to bed before he sparked up his first cigarette of the night and poured his first whisky. They shared a bed, but most of the time he would just fall into it unconscious. On nights when he wasn't drinking (those rare occasions) he would read a couple of pages of some trashy novel and that would force the sleep to come. He often faked it – the sleep, and would soberly lie there, his back to hers, feeling nothing, not really considering life after the birth of the child. It was as if it was happening to someone else. Someone who cared. He had gone along to the scans, found out they would be having a boy. He knew he should have been jumping with joy – a son! But nothing. But nothing happened, he just became encompassed by a feeling of disappointment. He had wanted them to say that it was a phantom, a bad case of indigestion.

He started to drink in front of her, not because he wanted to taunt her, because she couldn't, but because he needed to. He couldn't wait for her to go to bed. He needed that negative feeling as soon as he crossed the threshold of the house. It wasn't her, it wasn't him. It was the situation. For the first five months of the marriage he drowned himself in alcohol.

The labour came three weeks early. He was lying, drunk and unconscious on the settee, LPs and their covers strewn all over the floor as one click, click clicked at its end on the turntable. Sheila walked calmly down the stairs, her hospital bag in hand, and woke him. 'It's time.' That was all she had said. He felt himself sober up instantly and got to his feet, kicking over an ashtray as he did. 'Right, I'll drive, I'm fine. I'll be alright.' She drove. He sat in the passenger seat on the short drive to the hospital feeling more guilty than he ever had in his life.

She was calm. She parked in the car park and on the short walk to the maternity entrance she stopped and squatted by the kerb. He didn't want to look, but felt he should. What he saw wasn't normal, he knew that now. What he saw under the piercing hospital spotlights was brown liquid running down the hill back toward the main road. Sheila straightened up, and he stood useless, bag in hand awaiting instruction. She carried on walking towards the entrance and he offered his hand as support. She simply looked through him, the sheen from the spotlights making him opaque. He was nothing, a shadow, a drunken useless genie who had followed her here from the bottom of his bottle. She hobbled on and they entered the empty reception hall. Sheila pointed to the lifts and he dutifully walked towards them, his finger poised to press the button. 'Second floor,' she instructed him, her breath short.

The lift took its time coming, but when it did and they arrived on the second floor he felt even more useless than he had previously. A midwife, two nurses and a doctor quickly assessed the situation and told his wife (not him) than her glucosmia or some such word had burst – the child's bowels had opened – and the two of them were now in danger if she didn't give birth soon. He stood at the back as she got on to the bed and had the stirrups added. As the medical team gathered round her looking anxious and talking jargon to each other he tasted the fermented alcohol in his drying mouth. They explained to Sheila what they had to do – an epidural – and asked if she was okay with this. She nodded her consent and an anaesthetist was sent for. The nurse offered her gas and air and she accepted, breathing in deeply. Her eyes were smiling but as she pulled the mask away from her mouth she turned to him scornfully, a bitter smile on her lips. 'You wouldn't like this Robert, probably not strong enough for you.' She replaced the mask over her mouth and Steele watched as all the eyes in the room met his. He said nothing. As it was, two anaesthetists arrived and silently set about injecting something into the small of Sheila's back. They were talking, but it didn't seem to be aimed at any one in particular.

Steele's mouth felt like the bottom of a sandpit, but he was too embarrassed to even suggest that someone pass him the jug of water that was placed the other side of his wife's bed. He simply stood, wobbling slightly as his mouth closed, his lips feeling as though they'd been glued together. There was a flurry of movement and more white coats came unannounced through the door. It was a scene of controlled panic around his wife's splayed knees. He was escorted from the room by a nurse. He couldn't make out what she said, but from her grip on his elbow he surmised she could have been on the force. He knew all was not well.

Steele felt the van almost turn ninety degrees as it took a corner. He turned and looked at Mansell, his mouth seeming to bite at the tape. He wished he had the fight, the drive, but nothing. But nothing was all he had. Nothing but acceptance of his predicament. The van came to a halt. He needed to get back in the game. There was no more time for feeling sorry. He was in a fight for his life and the negativity needed shaking from his black brain. This was the time for… ha ha… Secret Affair, he thought, the time for action.

With the van at a standstill he was able to jolt himself round and face Mansell. He wriggled his hands and wrists in no uniform fashion, just twisted them this way and that until at last he could at least move them slightly. He was able to fish both his hands into his right-hand coat pocket, feeling for what he needed. He found it, he may have been prepared to give up on smoking, but smoking hadn't given up on him. He felt the embossed pattern on the side of his Zippo – Paisley, no less – and began the careful process of positioning it between the palms of his hand. The van jolted forward as he did so, but he scrabbled about on the floor and found it again and with both thumbs he lifted the lid and lit it under the seemingly solid tape that bound his wrists. It caught right away, and much to his chagrin, instead of burning straight up and releasing him from its' grip, the tape burnt in a circular manner as though following the threads of the material which had given it its' strength. He danced like a drunken dervish on the floor of the van as the heat of the flames burnt the hairs on his wrist and scorched at his skin. Five seconds later – it had felt more like hours – he snapped his wrists free of their taped and burning prison and pulled them round to the front of his body, pointlessly blowing on them. He sat up and quickly located the lighter and burnt the tape that bound his ankles into submission. Again the agony, but he was free.

He noticed that Mansell, still bound, was nodding towards his own coat pocket. Steele fished in it. A knife! A bloody Swiss Army knife! He remonstrated silently with him, as he nervously pulled at the tape that gagged his own mouth. It wasn't budging, so he pulled it in one fell swoop. 'Jesus Christ!' he squealed. 'Jesus! Jesus!' He theatrically shook his head from side to side as he opened Mansell's knife before cutting him loose. 'Remind me never to get a Brazilian. Think I've lost half my top lip.'

Mansell struggled to get the tape off his wrists and then his ankles. He then stood up and wished he hadn't. He clattered the top of his head on the roof of the van. Steele was about to laugh when all of a sudden, the two of them were thrown back to the floor as the van twisted a hundred and eighty degrees. It took them a couple of seconds – again they felt like hours – to realise that this wasn't part of their kidnapper's plan, this was a road traffic accident. They both hit the side wall of the van, protecting themselves as best they could as the van juddered to a halt. A couple of seconds after it had, Steele gingerly got to his feet and booted the back door of the vehicle open.

Through the gloom of the rain he stared outside. Stared at the windscreen of a black Astra, big red L on the roof. Inside a driving instructor was holding his balding head in his hands and beside him Harry Spencer was looking a tad sheepish. It was the best thing Steele had ever seen in his life and for the first time in years he smiled from ear to ear.

35

Sarinder Kapoor slapped Steele heartily on the back. 'You are like a new man DI Steele,' he sat down across from him. 'I heard all about your escapades with the McCulloch fellow. You've got them watertight in the cells and it has you smiling like a newlywed man.'

Steele remembered his time as a newlywed, but shook the thought loose and continued to smile. 'For the first time I feel lucky to be alive.'

'It is a good feeling, no?' Kapoor sniffed in the air.

'So, who you think is next on the hit list?' Kapoor asked the question as though asking Steele to pass the salt.

'I did think it was me, but some random junkies got found with some of my cards on them and coughed to that. So your guess is as good as mine.' Steele sat down heavily in his chair.

'And do you not think that he', Kapoor nodded vaguely in the direction of the cells, 'could be responsible for the two murders?'

'Nah,' Steele replied convincingly. 'This guy is something else, more than just a lowlife scumbag like McCulloch and his cronies.'

'Yes,' Kapoor nodded. 'I concur with your viewpoint. What he did was calculated, nothing random nor chaotic like you would expect with someone of McCulloch's ilk. Definitely, you are right.'

'I think he's just laughing at us, toying with us.' Steele added. 'I mean, two murders down. Who's next? Could be one of us. For all we know he might be following our every move and thinking that we're closing in on him, that he's cornered and the only way out is to come after one of us. You? Me? Mansell? Bain? The only trouble with that theory is that it's not true. If only he would come after one of us we would have some fucking clue as to where to look.'

'Too many red herrings, and not the big fish we are after,' Kapoor smiled.

Steele rolled his eyes. 'Get! You're no bloody help, you and your "old man and the sea" analogies. Red Herrings? Blind alleys more like. The police handbook, the unwritten version,' Steele wondered whether to continue, when he pontificated like this he cringed realising he was turning into his father. 'Anyway, plain and simple – unlawful death and you look close to home. Lover, relation, business partner, money lender, friend. So far – nothing except some homemade handjob of a DVD featuring a lot of overweight monstrosities in cardboard celebrity masks ploutering into the top divorce lawyer in Paisley. One of whom – Alisdair McCulloch we have in custody, but his alibi's as cast iron as Maid Marion's chastity belt.'

'Still,' Kapoor slapped him and made to exit. 'You have his young cousin bang to rights for the Gallowhill murder.'

'To use your parlance Sarinder,' Steele held the door open for him, 'He's small fry, a definite tiddler.'

Steele sat down at his desk and stared idly out the window at the council building. Oh what he'd give to be in Lah Lah Land right now.

36

He spread the paper in front of him. There he was again, front page and a full reminder of all his past inglorious failures on pages four and five. Jesus! When would he learn? This time the paper was trying to make him out to be some sort of idiot savant who had foiled the imminent execution of two police officers. He looked at the grainy photos of the officers. No doubt taken from out of date ID badges. He knew they looked nothing like that now – especially the older one. Old age doesn't come alone, he mused. Steele had obviously let his guard down, it was all there in black and white – His stuttering investigation into the murders of Georgina McBride and "our very own and sadly missed" Bob McLean, The assault in Central Way and, the piste de resistance – his own kidnap and near death experience at the hand of some local lowlife. Yes, his guard had definitely slipped, not as low as it would when he got a hold of him though. But that could wait, he was in no hurry to dispatch DI Robert Steele just yet. He could be the final piece in the jigsaw, give him time to try and establish what the picture on the front of the box was! God he was good, part of him wanted to get caught just so he could show off to the Mill Street Muppets exactly how and why he had taken them for a ride. He would love to see their eyes widen as finally the forty-watter in their heads gave a collective PING! Idiots. The world was full of them. No, Steele could wait. He knew who was next – the hardest of all, the one closest to home. If the clowns didn't figure out what was happening after this then they needed their warrant cards taken from them, melted down and to have the molten plastic dripped gently into their frustrated arseholes. That thought made him think of her. Number three, as she would now be known. Not a person, not sentient, just NEXT! He thought of her, Angie, the skank. Angie lying flat on the bed, lubed and telling him not to force it too soon. She had allowed him access to that darkest of places when Idiot Boy had refused to do it on the grounds that it was "too gay". Charlotte had slapped him when he had dared to venture his pinky finger in its' general direction. Angie was the only one he had ever done it with, the only one ever to allow him. He felt himself stiffen and lifted the paper and rose to his feet. He positioned it to the front of his trousers as he made his way to the toilet.

37

Blair Devine's eyed widened in disbelief as he read the words of praise The Paisley Daily Express were heaping upon Harry Spencer. So now he was a hero, just because he had wrecked his car and unwittingly released two kidnapped coppers. Now he was a hero? What about the murders? He was next, he knew he was next? How the hell could he stop himself from ending up on a steel tray in the morgue. Was keeping Spencer sweet the right idea? Was it any kind of idea at all? His thoughts were like knitted mince, he had no idea any more what in the name of God was happening to him. He lifted his mobile and dialled his home phone, even though he was in the kitchen. He heard the phone ring in the living room and knew no one would answer, no one else was in. He just let it ring, he was phoning in sick on himself! The envelope from The Procurator Fiscal's office sat unopened on the breakfast bar. He could see the headlines now "The Silverburn Sex Beast". He felt a wee stay at Hotel Dykebar coming on.

38

Steele couldn't believe what he was hearing. He had heard similar things like it twice before, but he hadn't expected it now. Now that he was in the eye of a hurricane of murders. 'I thought we had cleared all this up.'

'Transparency Bob,' Chief Inspector Bain sucked at his bottom lip. 'That's the name of the game these days.'

DI Rob Steele hated being called "Bob" by anyone, least of all by a Chief Inspector who had just told him he was being suspended pending an investigation into an "assault on a female member of the public in Paisley central post office at approximately 11.25 a.m. on Monday 13th of August." He couldn't contain his rage. 'With all due respect sir, fuck off!' he slammed his palm on the desk. 'Some wee junkie trollop accuses me of assault and all of a sudden it's hand in your badge sheriff. You're not on sir, I'm in the middle of one of the most serious investigations this town has known since...'

'BOB!' Bain boomed, his face crimson. 'If anyone's to "fuck off" it's you! Warrant card, NOW!' It was Bain's turn to slam the desk. 'It's not as though you were getting anywhere, all you've managed is to do is get yourself hospitalised and kidnapped. To say nothing of your contempt for one of the finest criminal minds that this countr...'

'Sanderson?' Steele gawped incredulously and saw the slight tinge of shame join the red on Bain's beetroot face. It was true, once you got to a certain level – whether you be good or evil – you're all in it together, looking down at the rest and frowning contemptuously. 'You're not telling me...'

'As for this shoe pervert!' Bain's idea of changing the subject was laughable. 'He's still out there Scot free!'

'Pathetic!' Steele sighed and took his warrant card from his inside jacket pocket and placed it on the desk. 'Absolutely pathetic. Sanderson accuses us and you're too scared to contradict him.'

'I'll be assigning McGlaughlin and Patterson to your caseload from now on.' Bain added.

Steele couldn't contain himself and laughed spontaneously. 'Good luck with that one.' With that he opened the door and walked towards the stairs. On the way down, he looked at his watch and was dismayed to find that it wasn't yet opening time.

39

The rain had at last abated, but all the cloud cover suggested it would be less than an hour until it returned again. The clouds suggested a late hour, but it was only after six. For Steele's body it felt like the Witching hour had been and gone. He had been drinking since eleven, only the occasional foray outside to smoke some guilt-tipped cigarettes breaking up his Guinness and whisky endeavours. He looked despairingly at the packet – four left – so much for giving up, again! He'd once been told it was a harder habit to chuck than the brown stuff, and as he sucked in the nicotine he wondered where the rush was, where was the hit? If it was harder to give up than heroin then surely there must be some initial buzz, some sky high hit that caused him to spend getting close to two grand a year on the bloody things! But there was nothing, just the satisfaction that he had apparently shortened his life by another five minutes and would die a slow and painful death. Happy days. He smoked in silence, ignoring the furtive glances from one of Bertie's regulars – a former body builder, intent now on polluting his "temple" with cancer rather than steroids. He stared at the tapas bar across the road, the waiter polishing glasses at the bar as the kitchen staff sat at an unfurnished table, obviously wondering if there would be any covers on a wet Wednesday in Paisley. Steele doubted it, the town needed something, but he didn't know what it was. All he knew was that he had been doing his bit for civic upkeep and where had it got him? Suspended and smoking outside a miserable, empty pub on a wet weekday. He took one last puff and tossed the snout in the gutter between two parked cars. He headed back inside, he was nowhere near drunk enough yet.

'Jesus!' Bertie started to pour him another Guinness without asking. 'You're your usual happy-go-lucky self. What's the matter? They run out of custard in the canteen before you got there.'

'Nothing that simple,' Steele didn't want to talk but found himself doing so. 'Suffice it to say, I won't be doing much detecting for a while, thanks to some skank head.'

'Is that right,' Bertie fished, letting half the pint settle. 'You wanting another half as well?'

Steele waved his hand in acquiescence. 'I mean, it's a bad day when you can't give a junky a slap without worrying as to how it will affect your employment arrangements.'

'Aye,' Bertie agreed. 'I'd shoot the bloody lot of them.'

'It's not like she was actually hurt,' Steele continued. 'It's just the compo she's after, pure and simple. Not a thing on CCTV either, but all the folk on the hill worry about is bad publicity – pay her off and keep her quiet.'

'She? Like?' Bertie's brow furrowed.

'He? She? Doesn't matter, they're the same animal, aren't they?' Steele rested his elbows on the bar. 'Maybe there should be a season for it, like the glorious twelfth for the grouse. There's an idea.'

'And not a bad one if you ask me,' Bertie placed the Guinness beside his left elbow. 'Grouse, is it?' he smiled.

'Pertinent,' Steele nodded his head. 'A wee low flyer, a double. You want one yourself?'

'Don't worry about that,' Bertie answered. 'I get plenty as it is.' It was true, he never left a shift without at least eight cans of lager and a half bottle. It was no crime, it was his to steal, after all. 'So, have they got anyone for that girl's murder?'

'Nope,' answered Steele. 'And at this rate they're not likely to. The trail will be stone cold.'

'What about that old reporter?' asked Bertie. 'The guy from across the road?' He pointed out to New Street and The Express offices. 'Sounds like there's a right nutter on the loose.'

'Aye, "a right nutter", would sum it up.' Steele smiled, it was something a treasured uncle might say about his strange neighbour, not about someone who had killed then mutilated two human beings. 'I don't know Bertie,' he sighed. 'There's a part of me that's glad I've nothing to do with it anymore, but you know that way that when you start a job you want to see it through to the end? It's like that. Should be used to it though, get swapped over all the time on jobs, but never on one this serious.'

'They don't believe in continuity,' Bertie smirked. 'Or agree with slapping junkies? What is the world coming to?' He cackled and found a pint glass to polish with his cloth.

Steele smiled, and fished in his pocket. Would now be a good time to call Mansell? Find out if he was any further forward? Probably not, but he took out his phone anyway and made the call. As it was ringing he stepped outside. There were no pleasantries, 'Any news Dave?'

Mansell was taken aback, he was using his first name. 'Well,' he paused, knowing what he was about to say would irk his former colleague greatly. 'He's taken me off the case as well sir,' He couldn't help himself "sir"! This was just some random person he was speaking to, a man that was no longer his boss.

'What?' Steele felt about in his pocket for his pack of cigarettes, but saw he had left them on the bar counter.

'That's right,' Mansell sounded angry, an emotion he rarely used. 'I'm on the important case now – The Shoe Pervert!'

'Jesus Christ!' Steele was almost speechless. 'What is it with this thing and our Chief Inspector? He does realise it's a shoe sniffer and not a shoe bomber we're looking for?' He laughed, wishing he had said that at the time he was being carpeted and hadn't thought about it eight hours later in a drunken haze.

'He's put The Two John's on the case?' Mansell knew this would annoy Steele.

'Fuck me! The dream team!' Steele didn't want to steal Mansell's thunder by telling him he knew all this already.

'Exactly,' Mansell had more. 'They've arrested Spencer again, charged him, again!'

'That's it?' Steele was flabbergasted. 'They think that's it? Beat a confession out of that idiot and watch the crime figures fall? What happens when he strikes again? What then, eh? Arseholes.'

'I know,' Mansell agreed. 'I'm thinking of putting in a transfer request, going back to Pitt Street, things were more coherent over there, wasn't about who you know or your face fitting.'

'Or which DI you were assigned to,' Steele added, feeling guilty. 'You're getting bumped by association, not because you're a bad polis. You're going places son, you've just had a bad placement – with me. The likes of McGlaughlin and Patterson will be plodding all their days, but not you. Stick it out for the moment Dave, there needs to be someone in Mill Street who believes we still have a maniac on the loose. Those clowns will be cracking open the champers as we speak.'

'No doubt sir,' Mansell was blushing, Steele had never spoken to him (or anyone) like that before. 'I'll see how long I can hack it sir, but I can't promise anything.'

'See you son,' Steele clicked the phone off, not waiting for a reply and went back into the bar to fetch his cigarettes. 'It's alright,' he shouted over to Bertie. 'The murder enquiry's in the bag – They've got Laurel and Hardy on the case.' He turned towards the door, intent on smoking himself into an early grave.

40

Angela James and her son Marley sat in the council building waiting for their number to come up. She looked despairingly at the green "deli-style" ticket in her hand, another four in front of her. She had already been waiting thirty-five minutes and found the recalcitrant staff less than warm to her plea that she had a life to be getting on with. They seemed to take great pleasure in making people wait. And wait. And wait, until every ounce of spark and spirit had been sapped from their bodies. Bodies that had been initially filled with rage when they had entered through the slower than usual revolving door. Bodies filled with rage that the council – as usual – had cocked something up, sent out the wrong bill, posted unnecessarily harsh reminder notices for pittances. The effects of the heavily loaded joint with which she had greeted the brand new day was wearing off and she felt her own brittle joints rub angrily against each other. She was due her methadone at Lloyds in twenty minutes and she could almost taste the sweet green nectar on her tongue. She was distracted by her son swinging his legs on the end of the plastic less than fantastic chair and she slapped him on the arm. 'Stop fidgeting Marley,' she scowled. 'You're doing my head in.'

The boy said nothing, simply shuffled in his seat rubbing his arm and scowling at his mother. He knew better than to do any more than that in the morning, before she had visited her "doctors" to get her medicine. Mornings she was grumpy, afternoons she was asleep and at night he just stayed in his room away from the men and women who filled his living room with smoke and mistrust.

Angie's number, 245, flashed up on the display board, followed by "go to information point 4". Instinctively she looked at the green ticket in her hand, even though she was sure of the number – she had been repeating it in her head for the past half hour, trying to keep herself from exploding with pain and rage. She grabbed at Marley's arm and hauled him to his feet. 'Come on you.' She walked toward booth 4.

'How, can, I, help, you, mad, madam?' the assistant asked her.

Angie's eyes narrowed, sure the boy was taking the piss. Why was his language so punctuated? Was he trying to tell her he thought she was slow? Was he getting wide? Her paper cut eyes caught his – dopey and doe-like, and scanned down to his face, still dotted with the deep scars of teenage acne, which, like his shyness, refused to budge. Angie sat herself down and pulled the council-headed letter from her pocket. 'It's this,' she threw the letter towards him and smiled internally as he visibly flinched. 'He doesn't live with me anymore, so I'm due my rebate back, so I want you to sort it.'

The boy held the letter and his eyes focussed on the writing. It took him a minute and a half to read through its contents and all the while he could hear the angry breathing of the customer in front of him. 'So, you, are, Angela, Jame, James?'

'Obviously,' she snarled back.

'And, this, is, your, address, thir, thir, teen, Fitz, fitz, alan Dri, Drive?'

'Aye, aye.' She barked.

'It's, just, for, the, sys, system,' he typed nervously at the keyboard. 'All, your, information, will, be, stored, in, here, and, we, can, adjust, it, accord, accordingly.'

'Listen pal, no offence,' she squinted to see the name on his ID badge, 'Edward, but is there any chance I could see somebody else? I've got appointments to keep and I can see this taking all day.'

'I, can, assure, you, miss, James, that, I, am, more, than, capable, of, dealing, with, your, enquiry, timeously, and, accurate, accurately.' Edward felt a tap on his left shoulder and as he turned he gulped.

'It's okay,' the blond man squinted to see the name on his ID badge, 'Edward. I'll deal with this. You go and have a coffee break.'

Edward was numb, this was the first time *he* had ever spoken to him, and he knew his name. 'No, prob, problem, mist, mister...' Before he had the chance to finish the blond man had ushered him away from the customer service desk.

'On you go,' The blond man told him. 'Have a break.' When he was sure he was out of earshot he spoke to the customer. 'Hello Angie. Long-time no see.'

It had taken Angie until now to realise who he was. 'You?' she said bitterly.

'That's right,' he sat down opposite her. 'Me.'

'What do you want?'

He picked up the letter from the desk and gave it a cursory glance. 'These things, these problems you have. I can make them disappear like that.' He clicked his fingers like he was beckoning a hapless waiter. 'But first I need you to do something for me.'

'That'll be right,' she scowled.

'Yes, Angela dear,' he smiled. 'That will be right.'

41

Steele stared desolately at the spirits on the shelf in his kitchen. Never again he kept telling himself. Never again because it was doing nothing for him, a bit like the cigarettes. The spirits neither buoyed nor saddened him, he merely passed out and felt terrible in the morning. Once more he had awoke to find almost his whole collection of vinyl decorating the carpet in his living room. He turned his attention away from the spirits and poured himself a pint of cold water from the tap. He saw it off in two gulps before filling his empty glass and going through to the living room and his scattered records. He made his way through them and sat on the chair by the window. He instinctively turned on the TV and waited for the picture to appear. When the pixels settled he spluttered a mouthful of water at the screen. There staring back at him was Chief Inspector Bain, his rotund face filling the whole of the twenty-four-inch screen. When he spoke he seemed to be forgetting to breath out and his face seemed to be inflating. Steele scowled and moved in closer to the screen to listen to his former boss.

"This is just a short statement to let the good people of Paisley know that they can rest easy in their beds once more and we have apprehended the perpetrator of the murders of both Georgina McBride and Bob McLean. As you can appreciate we have a number of questions to ask this man before officially charging him, but you can be confident that," he paused and smirked straight to camera, **"like the Canadian Mounties, we've definitely got our man. Any questions at this time would obviously prejudice any case against the accused, so as…"**

"Is it true that the man in custody is Harry Spencer? Erstwhile referred to as "Frank" due to his proclivity to make a fool of himself in public?" a reporter's voice interrupted.

'Don't say a word,' Steele muttered at the screen. 'Do not say another fuc...'

"As I said any answers I give would prejudice the CPS's case," Bain smirked, smirked and gave the whole game away. "Needless to say, we're very confident we have our man. No more questions gentlemen, and lady."

Steele's thumb bumped down angrily on the red off switch and he threw the remote control to the other side of the room. 'Idiots! What a bunch of useless fuc...' his ranting was interrupted by the ringing of his phone. He answered it on the second ring.

'I take it you were watching that?' the voice on the other side of the line sounded as awe-struck as he was. It was Mansell.

'Jesus!' Steele sat back in his chair. 'What was he thinking? *Was* he thinking?'

'It's a mess sir,' sighed Mansell. 'Everyone in the station's celebrating, there's every chance there'll be bunting hanging in the reception desk by the afternoon. They've made a complete arse of it.'

'You don't say.'

'Word is that McGlaughlin broke his hand getting the confession out of him. He's walking about like Mike Tyson, dragging what's left of his knuckles on the ground. When he's not kissing them, that is.'

'So, have you put your request in?' asked Steele.

'Yes,' Mansell answered. 'But Bain thinks he's being noble by not accepting it straight off. Says he wants me to clear up some loose ends first.'

'What loose ends?'

'The shoe weirdo.' Mansell almost laughed. 'He's obsessed. I think I'll just get McGlaughlin or Patterson to slap our boy Spencer another couple of times, plant some stilettos on him.'

Steele spied the almost empty bottle of whisky by the other chair and exhaled loudly. 'There's some loose ends I need to clear up as well. Are you with me?'

'You've got to let it go sir,' Mansell appealed to him. 'Let them make their usual pig's ear of it and laugh up your sleeve when the CPS decide there's not enough evidence for it to go to court.'

'Meantime, the real killer's free to mutilate his next victim as Mill Street parties. No, I'm going to be all over it. We've been looking at it from the wrong angle. It'll be something simple, something so glaringly obvious that we'll boot ourselves in the backside for not having spotted it sooner.' Steele stopped, the other end of the line quieter than it should be. 'Are you there son?' he asked meekly.

'Yes sir, I'm here,' Mansell sighed. 'What time do you want me to pick you up?'

'That's the spirit son,' Steele almost felt like cheering. 'Half an hour should see me washed and dressed.'

42

Mansell drove his car to the car park in the sky and parked up facing the Clyde Valley – probably one of the best views of the West of Scotland accessible by car. It was a surprisingly bright and crisp autumnal day and the two men shared a communal sigh as Mansell switched off the engine.

'Would almost make you believe in some kind of God,' Steele stated looking out at the wonder.

'Aye, it would,' Mansell muttered somewhat inaudibly. He had made up his own mind on the existence of "some kind of God" at the birth of his first daughter, but he knew better than to share his thoughts on childbirth with Steele.

'But then you get events like we've been having the past wee while would lead you to believe there was nothing in this world but pure evil.' Steele commented.

'In Paisley at least,' agreed Mansell.

'Paisley sneezes on a Saturday and by Sunday the rest of the world has a cold,' Steele laughed.

'Not like you to be so philosophical,' Mansell lifted an eyebrow. 'It's the macabre aspects of the murders that are getting to me, the mutilation afterwards. Is it not just enough to kill? But to have to deface them when they can do nothing about it, feel nothing about it. That's just...'

'That's just for our benefit,' Steele interjected. 'He sees himself as a big cat and we're just the wee wounded mouse that he's playing with. He sees us as nothing, no respect for the police.'

'Who has these days?' sighed Mansell.

'And therein lies our problem,' stated Steele. 'There's too much out there,' he waved a hand over the landscape. 'Too many cop shows, too much information on the internet, too much for people to take in. They see that everybody else has got such a fantastic life and they want it. People can't be content with what they have. Content with the hand that they're dealt. More, more, more. (how do you like it? how do you like it? more, more, more.) Let's get out and stretch our legs.'

'I'd swear you were still pissed,' laughed Mansell as he slammed the door closed. 'You don't talk this much garbage when your sober.' He felt confident talking to Steele like this now, nothing to do with his former boss's suspension, but he was the only one, the only one in Mill Street who seemed in any way human. The rest just kept their noses and shoes clean and made sure their balance sheets totted up at the end of the day. Steele seemed simply to exist, working away without anyone noticing, neither bragging nor berating himself. It was only since he had been forced out that he actually saw what monsters the others were, the distinction between good and evil being a very fine line, their definition of evil a matter of conjecture.

'The trick is never to get too sober,' Steele smiled across the roof of the car. 'What's the point in getting sober, when you'll only get drunk again?' he crooned tunelessly.

Mansell shook his head. 'You couldn't carry a tune in a bucket.' He looked around at the other cars, not suspiciously, before zapping the car closed. 'Where to now?' he asked.

'That way,' Steele pointed in the general direction of The Paisley Golf Club at the top of Braehead Road. 'It's not a hike, mind. Just a general stroll to clear the head.'

'But my head's…'

'Just walk son, just walk.'

43

'It's my own fault,' Blair Devine rocked back and forth on the side of his bed, his hands seemingly glued to his thighs. 'I should have been a good boy. *Leave the girls Blair, leave the girls alone*. I'll be good Mammy, promise. Promise Mammy, Blair wants to play with the girls. Please Mammy. Blair will be a good boy. Please Mammy.'

Blair had driven himself round in circles, literally. He had got in his car and driven the circuit through Barrhead town centre and down the road towards The Hurlet where he turned left and ripped down the dual carriageway and the Dkyebar Road the mental hospital stood on. He passed the first time at fifty-five, not wanting to look in, fearing he would see demonic towers and mad scientists enacting bizarre experiments on the vulnerable. He cut a left down Blackbriars Road and then towards The Hurlet and the dual carriageway once more, before leaving the roundabout at the first junction and heading up the hospital road again. He slowed to forty, the building itself looked like red sandstone, warm and inviting. It was set in a tree-filled park – tranquil. He went past though and did the Blackbriars/Hurlet/dual carriageway circuit once more. He did that circuit fourteen times before, on the last of them, stopping his car in the road and getting out without switching off the engine, much to the annoyance of the drivers behind him. An oncoming bus had to break to miss him as he blindly crossed the road and walked through the perimeter gates and into the hospital grounds. It wasn't so bad, there were no guards with guns or dogs, no sirens or floodlights, no high barbed-wire fences. He simply walked in and began to discard his clothing as he walked towards the building. Polo shirt, vest, chinos, boxers, he kept his shoes and plain white socks on, he wasn't mad. By the time he reached the building there was a party waiting to meet him, his impromptu striptease had created quite a stir on the wards and a couple of friendly orderlies and a female doctor were there to greet him. They gave him a hospital gown and invited him in.

He had never been in a mental institution before, had only ever seen them in films, "One Flew Over the Cuckoo's Nest" and suchlike. This place was nowhere near as grim as that, not a nurse Rachet in sight and no need to throw porcelain sinks through the windows.

'Leave the girls Blair, leave the girls alone!' He felt the hospital issue gown run up his thighs as he rubbed continuously. He deserved what was happening to him. He deserved Spencer to be coming after him, his very own avenging angel, out to right the wrongs his body and soul had committed against the girls.

Blair Devine rocked back on forth on the side of his bed. He was broken. They had left him on his own to calm down, there were no jags to the arse or unnecessary sedation. This should have calmed him, but didn't, it just gave him more time to think about his failings and mistakes. He had sent out the DVDs to all the perverts he had recognised at the Renfrewshire Rope & Twine Co, but had forgotten to post his blackmail letters, he had found them in the drawer of his desk in his back bedroom – his office, awaiting mailing before he had left the house this morning. It was the easiest thing in the world – include a letter in each envelope, but he had failed. He had failed at something that simple, something a child could have achieved. He deserved Spencer to come after him, to kill him. If only to put him out of his misery.

44

Was it just too easy, or was he just too good? Too good for this town, this country, this existence even. There was nobody, no body and nothing could touch him. They were way too stupid, way too locked into their own trivialities to see that he was their very own Geppetto. They stepped out of line and he showed them. He tugged at their strings and extinguished their meagre, meaningless lives. Angela. Sweet, sweet, sourly sweet Angela. She thought he loved her, that he wanted to help. To improve her pointless life and that of her bastard son. The boy? The boy would no doubt talk. But there was nothing that could be done about that. He couldn't kill a child. Could he? What sort of monster would that make him? That would only attract attention, he laughed out loud at the thought that he hadn't already created "a bit of a stir". He couldn't believe the afterwards though. Normally the "afterwards" of any kind of sex was a cuddle and a smoke, instead he had turned his hand to butchery. Buggery and butchery, he laughed, he should write this down for his memoirs. The amount of blood was much worse though, much more uncontrollable than the previous two. They had been streams compared to the ocean of blood that had spewed from Angela's, dear sweet, sourly sweet Shireen... her heavily engorged manto, her heavily plump hooten... He really should be writing some of this down, this wasn't specks of shiny dust, this was gold, platinum even. He didn't have time though, getting cleaned up was his priority.

He looked down as the pellets of water from the shower beat on his manhood and felt it come to life again at the thought. So soon? He thought of Angela and her unlubricated fat arse. He squirted some gel from the bottle onto his hand and it headed south.

45

Detective Chief Inspector Bain was no use at looking contrite, he hadn't had the practice. The kind of family he came from, you were either right or you kept your mouth shut. You never pretended, never bullshitted. 'I'm sorry Robert,' he held out his hand, 'These developments show categorically that you were right when you questioned the veracity of Spencer's arrest and guilt.'

'His former partner murdered and mutilated by someone with the same M.O. whilst he was in the care of H.M. Constabulary Mill Street kind of makes it hard to question his innocence,' Steele couldn't help himself.

'The other matter though,' it was Bain's turn not to help himself – the bugger wasn't getting off Scot-free. 'Punching a member of the public.' He smiled internally, but his lips remained sternly thin. 'That will have to be investigated, obviously after we've cleared up this nasty business.'

Nasty business? Steele had to hold back a laugh. A lawyer with her tongue almost sliced off, a journalist – Bob – (Bob had a face, Bob had a life, Bob had a drink with him.) with his fingers held onto his knuckle by flapping skin and now this, the former lover of Harry Spencer and cause of all his troubles buggered, murdered and had her... He couldn't get the thought out of his head, thankfully he hadn't seen it, but "nasty business" barely did it justice. 'I know sir,' Steele had to get back on track, no time for reprisals or silly feuds with colleagues. 'I know D.S. Mansell has requested a transfer, but I think I could bring him round, even if it was just for this case. Do you mind if I phone him?'

'I'll do it,' Bain coughed uncomfortably, 'I'll let him know you're back at the helm.'

Steele disguised his smile, already having phoned Mansell, already having primed him to act surprised. 'We need to get the boy to talk. Marley?'

'Yes,' Bain concurred. 'Poor little sod. Imagine having to witness...' Bain's large fist beat against the side of his overblown right thigh. 'We've got to catch this bastard Rob,' he hissed. 'That boy, what that boy must have had to have seen...'

'We'll get him sir,' interrupted Steele. 'If the social worker assigned is having trouble getting him to talk, then we need to get another one. Maybe even...' he sighed, knowing what he was about to say was going to baulk with Bain, but it needed to be said. 'Maybe even get Harry Spencer to sit in on the interview,' he paused as Bain looked as though he had been happy slapped by a group of schoolboys. 'He does seem to love the boy sir, and with all due respect, that's maybe what he needs right now, a friendly face, not some strange do-gooders filling him full of lies. He needs to grieve with someone who actually knows what he's going through.'

'What about the boy's biological father?' Bain clutched at his last straw, Spencer had been a monkey on his back for long enough now and he wanted rid of him.

'By all accounts he's unknown,' Steele replied. 'The result of Angela James's one and only visit to the wonderful city of Amsterdam. He knows nothing of Marley's existence.'

'You've done your homework Rob,' Bain sighed, realising he had been done up like an Arbroath Smokie. 'Do what you have to, I'll phone Mansell. That will be all.'

'Cheers sir.'

'Cheers Rob.'

46

Mansell took his seat in the interview room across from Harry Spencer and Marley James. Harry had his arm round the boy, both were sobbing incessantly. He wondered what was keeping Steele. He was uncomfortable with grief, especially the grief of a child, it was something he felt he would never get used to. Some did, saw it in the same way they did cracking a code, but he didn't have much time or much to do with the automatons on the force, he only dealt with humans. 'Won't be long,' he said apologetically. His words fell on deaf ears, the sobbing drowning them out. He rose from his chair and instinctively pushed it into the table. 'I'll just see what's keeping D.I. Steele.' He left the room and as he made to make his way down the corridor Steele came out of the room next door. 'What's keeping you sir?' he asked.

'Nothing,' he replied obtusely.

Mansell was flustered. 'They've been in there a good fifteen minutes and you've not sh...'

'And they've both been greeting like birthday cards for that fifteen minutes,' Steele raised his eyebrows. 'When they stop bubbling then we can go in and start with the good cop, good cop, until then come in here and pull up a pew.' he held open the door to the office next door to interview room four. Inside Mansell found Chief Inspector Bain staring at the monitor from the cameras intently. 'Sir.'

'Take a seat,' Bain instructed. 'Steele's right, there was no need for you to be in there.'

Well somebody could have told me! he felt like replying, but he knew better.

'There's nothing going to come when they're both in that state. It was just in case they said something,' Bain looked him in the eye. 'Thought we better have a man in there, make it legal, watertight. We hadn't abandoned you.' he spoke as though he and Steele had been sharing some private joke.

'Would we?' Steele sat beside him, grin on his face. 'Abandon our wee boy to the big bad wolves?' he spoke like he would to a child.

Mansell said nothing in reply, and the three men sat with their heads in their hands watching Harry Spencer and Marley James bawl their eyes out. It was another twenty minutes until their tears were dry. Steele and Mansell rose as one. 'You bring the tea and juice son,' he said to Mansell. 'I'll go in and see how the land lies.'

Steele waited for Mansell to come with the drinks before switching on the machine and introducing those present. 'I understand this is very difficult for you Marley but we need to try and find the man that did this to your mummy. Did you see him?'

All eyes were on the boy. The boy's eyes were on his shoes. He nodded.

'For the purposes of the tape Marley James nodded in acquiescence.' Mansell said.

Acquiescence? Steele thought, wanting to say something. 'Do you think you could tell us what he looked like?'

Again, the boy nodded but said nothing.

'Again, for the pu...' Steele put his hand across Mansell's mouth.

'It's okay, we'll wait until he says something.'

'If you want you can tell me,' Steele told him. 'Or if you'd rather tell...' Steele struggled. What would the boy call Spencer? Daddy number 2? Uncle Harry? He looked into Spencer's eyes for an answer.

'If you want to tell me Marley,' Spencer whispered softly. 'Then I can tell the policeman.'

Marley nodded again and Steele threw Mansell a look with "acquiesce" written all over it. Mansell remained silent.

'Was he tall Marley?' asked Steele.

The boy found Harry Spencer's ear and whispered into it. Spencer's face drained of all colour. 'Say that again Marley.' he spoke firmly to the boy as though scolding him. The boy looked to Steele and Mansell both of whom looked quizzically at Spencer.

'If the boy's said something Mr. Spencer then...' Steele was interrupted by Spencer shouting.

'Say that again Marley. Say that again!' Spencer roared angrily.

The boy looked terrified, once more on the verge of tears. 'It was uncle Ross,' he cried.

'Uncle Ross?' asked Steele, noticing Spencer was on the verge of a total collapse. He said it again. 'Uncle Ross?'

'My brother!' shouted Spencer. 'My fucking brother! I'll fucking kill him. I'll fucking kill him!'

'But why?' asked Mansell.

'The abuse, remember, at The Village? Ages ago?' Spencer's voice had risen an octave, he was raging. 'I was in the papers as one of the whistle-blowers, and he never forgave me. Said I had brought shame on him and that everybody was looking at him differently now that they all knew what had happened to him.'

'I see,' Steele nodded.

'We were kids,' Spencer sobbed. 'We didn't ask for it to happen, but he just felt we should have distanced ourselves from the whole thing, acted like it never happened. As if we were somehow asking for it.'

'As you say,' Steele's brow furrowed. 'It was ages ago, so why should he suddenly bring it to mind again?'

'Well, I'm in the papers again,' Spencer snorted, 'in case you didn't notice. He's ashamed of me and this is how... this is how...' Spencer's head dropped to the desk and he wept uncontrollably.' Harry Spencer placed his arm round the shoulder of Marley James and squeezed for all he was worth.

Steele and Mansell left the room.

47

'So how do we play it sir?' asked Mansell. He diverted his attention from the window and looked at his boss. His eyes had been fixed, staring at the council building across the way from them.

'Look at him,' Steele waved a hand at the window. 'Right under our bloody noses.' He stared hard at the blond man in the office – Ross Spencer - as he again berated someone on the telephone. 'I've seen him every day for the last... I don't know how long, little realising I was staring at... Jesus! This is a mess.'

'It's a bit ironic we kept pulling in the wrong brother,' sighed Mansell.

'Hilarious,' agreed Steele, tongue in cheek. 'And as to how we play it? I've absolutely no idea. All we've got is that boy's word, that'll never stick. We need physical evidence from him, match it up with what we've got and then nail the bastard to the wall. No stone left unturned. We'll follow him day and night, get together a couple of folk we can trust. But we need to keep it quiet for now, we don't want every dick in the village to charge in to try and be the hero that caught the beast. Softly softly, catchy monkey.'

Mansell squinted, his eyes focussing through the many droplets of rain on the window.

Steele noticed his discomfort. 'If you've any better ideas?' He was being genuine, and Mansell knew it.

'Well,' Mansell paused, his right hand rubbing at the back of his neck. 'It just seems a bit...well, not very pro-active. Tracking him, watching him. Why don't we let him know we're on to him, stick right on his tail and watch him crack up, hand himself to us on a plate. At least that way we can be certain he won't try and snuff anyone else out, he'll be too busy panicking.'

The two men stood in silence, Steele ruminating on what he had just heard. 'I like it. Get the bastard sweating. We'll do it your way. In the meantime, get a couple of uniforms together, bring them here and I'll brief them. Good thinking son.'

Mansell left the room and Steele stared in disbelief. 'Right under our bloody noses,' he muttered. 'I've spent too long wondering who you where,' he breathed heavily into the window. 'All this because your brother told the truth. Told the truth and made you look bad.' His index finger traced the path of a droplet of rain.

48

A mile and a half to the south of where Steele was staring out his window, Blair Devine was looking blankly out of his. He was doped right up to his vacant eyeballs. His finger too traced a raindrop, but somewhere in the process he lost track of it. It was too difficult, he had no concentration for it at all. It was taking him all his efforts to drool and dribble. After his initial evaluation he was prescribed a couple of milligrams of diazepam three times daily.

There was a quiet knock at the door before a woman in her early thirties entered, dressed safely, black office trousers, white blouse under a black cardigan pulled across her chest. Blair noticed she wore flat black mules on her feet.

'Blair?' She said softly. 'I'm Sarah. I've been assigned as your psychologist. Do you think you would be up for a little chat?'

Blair nodded his compliance, and sat down on the bed, leaving a space for her to sit.

She looked at him slightly uncomfortably. 'I was thinking more that we could go down to my office. Would that be alright?' Her life, she knew, was made up of questions asked. Asked and rarely replied with any degree of satisfaction.

'Mmm,' Blair walked slowly towards her, his spirit dragging behind.

Sarah let him pass and walk in front down the corridor, wary, as always, of the crack to the back of the head. It had happened once. She had been stupid once. She didn't expect it to happen again. 'Are you okay using the stairs?'

Blair nodded.

'Just down here then,' she held out her right arm and pointed to the double doors of the stairwell.

In contrast to the battleship grey corridors, Sarah's office was buzzing with life. She had chosen the colour scheme herself, azure blue walls and plush brown leather seats to sit and stare from, plants to talk to and a couple of large framed photographs of soft, warm beaches and crisp green oceans. Her piece-de-resistance, the ceiling was painted with "big fluffy clouds" – her secret throwback to her wild student days when she had partied just as hard as the rest of them, The Orbital song being her favourite come down tune. 'Have a seat Blair,' she tapped the back of one of the chairs. 'Make yourself comfortable.'

'Mmm.' Blair sat down, his bony bum barely touching the leather, his hunched frame forcing his bald head into his hands.

Sarah sat down opposite him, no notepad, she would write it up later, her brief experience having told her that nobody liked to be written about without being able to read what had been written. She held up the Dictaphone. 'Is it okay to record this?'

'Mmm,' Blair nodded. 'It's fine.'

Great! Sarah's brain boomed, it speaks! Now we were getting somewhere. 'So, Blair. When you came in,' she paused and cleared her throat. 'You were naked, stripping off. Is this...' She stopped, seeing Blair's head shaking involuntarily from side to side.

'I'm not bad,' he started, sitting back further into the chair. 'I'm not bad, they say I am. He thinks I am.'

'Who thinks you are Blair?' Sarah stuttered, having forgotten to switch on the machine.

'Them, the police, my mother, the papers. HIM!' He scowled.

'Who is "he" Blair?' Sarah asked. 'Is it your dad?' She was sure she was on the right track. So soon, so soon.

Blair smiled and snorted, liquid escaping his nostrils. 'My dad?' he made it sound so ridiculous. 'He's nothing like my dad. It's Spencer.' He waited for her response, but she just sat silently. 'The serial killer?' he added.

'What "serial killer" Blair?' she asked. 'Spencer who?'

'Not "Spencer who"!' he sounded raging. 'Harry Spencer. Killed that lawyer, then the reporter?'

Something in Sarah's head clicked and all at once she felt worried, her eyes glancing casually to the panic strip on the wall. 'And why does he think you're bad?'

'The money that I took from him,' replied Blair, calming slightly.

'What money is this?'

'For his lessons.' Blair sat right back in the chair now and looked at Sarah.

Now she was concerned. Lessons? For what? She coughed. 'What lessons?'

'Driving lessons,' he snapped back. 'I'm a driving instructor! Seventeen years and now he's haunting me. I'm next on his list. You've got to keep me here until they catch him.'

Sarah couldn't contain the puzzled expression on her face. She remembered it all now. She remembered Spencer from the photograph. From the photograph with Blair stood next to him. The whole town was alive with the talk of the deaths and these two – Spencer in particular – had been hailed a hero. Hailed a hero and then arrested a couple of days later. As far as she knew the police had him. 'Blair,' She leant forward, careful not to show too much cleavage, pulling the cardigan together again. 'They've caught him. Caught Spencer, it was on the news. Didn't you see it on TV?' She had no idea he had been released again, no one did, the police had a twenty-four-hour embargo on that particular piece of embarrassing news.

'I don't believe you,' Blair's face reddened. 'You're not lying to me are you?'

'No. He can't harm you, they've arrested him.'

'But they've done that before and let him out. They can't make anything stick. He seems daft as a brush, but he's giving them the run-around.' His head started shaking from side to side again. 'He's too clever for them.'

'Has he tried to harm you Blair?' she was puzzled, why hadn't he stopped the lessons instead of being photographed with his nemesis. 'Has he said anything?'

Blair shook his head. 'No. That's where he's clever.'

'Surely he wouldn't want to do you harm.' She tried to reassure him. 'After all, you were trying to help him learn to drive.'

'I'm sure he knows though,' Blair spoke incoherently. 'He knows.'

'What does he know?' asked Sarah.

'About the girls.' Blair's whole body appeared to retreat into the seat as the words left his mouth, like Ronnie Corbett on an over-sized chair.

Sarah wasn't sure she wanted to hear any more. Too much too soon might set him back, destroy any chance of complete recovery. 'Maybe we can talk about that the next time?' she suggested.

Blair, seeing she looked flustered, sat forward. 'It's nothing bad. It's just their shoes. Just their shoes, nothing bad.'

49

Steele and Mansell had been following Ross Spencer since he had left the council building, his mane of blond hair making him impossible to lose. He had gone straight from his work, through the grounds of the Abbey and towards County Square, where he had entered each one of the three bookies situated next to each other, without seemingly having a bet or any repartee with the staff. He left the last of them and walked over to the railway station entrance to The Last Post – generic non-music playing pub that had previously been the town's post office. Steele allowed Mansell to follow him, as he waited at the other entrance for what he was sure was about to happen. He timed it. Twenty-three seconds later, Ross Spencer and his blond mane exited at the other end of the former post office. He turned to the right, heading for yet another bookies. Steele smiled, the local paper had dubbed this area "little Vegas" when the last of the bookies had opened. Mansell appeared out the door to the pub, questions in his eyes.

'He's up there,' Steele nodded towards the bookies. 'What kept you? Did you have a sly pint?'

Mansell just pursed his lips in response and turned to see Ross Spencer walk to Moss Street and disappear into Betfred.
'Quite right,' Steele said to him. 'If you ask me, they should turn that place back into a post office. More life.'
'What's he playing at?' asked Mansell.
'Either he's a really indecisive gambler with a drinking problem,' Steele suggested. 'Or he's clocked us. My money's on the latter. We'll stalk him a while longer then get a couple of uniforms to follow him home. Get them to sit outside all night, do wonders for the neighbourhood watch committee, get those curtains twitching.' They had gleaned that Ross Spencer lived with

his wife and two sons in Elderslie – a very committed Neighbourhood Watch community. They had no idea his marital bliss had crumbled.

Spencer exited the fourth bookies, again apparently without having a bet, and smiled at the two policemen as they stood as conspicuously as they possibly could, standing against the window of a closed tobacconist. Steele smiled back whereas Mansell's expression remained fixed, still trying to give the impression that he wasn't following the suspect.

Upon seeing the returned smile, Spencer got bold, and walked across the cobbled street towards Steele and Mansell. 'Excuse me gents,' he opened. 'I can't help but get the feeling that you two are following me. If so, can I help you with anything?'

He was too cocky, too smug, Steele hated him instantly – his handsome tanned face, cheekbones to the fore, well-toned torso and confident attitude. What was there not to hate? He kept his vitriol in check through gritted teeth, his expression turning to surprise at the suggestion. 'No, we're not following you,' Steele frowned. 'Why would *we* be following you?'

'I was asking myself the same question,' Spencer started in a superior manner. 'Why would two foot police be following me? An upright, tax-paying citizen. I can't figure it out.'

'Police?' Steele snorted. 'Piss off!'

This threw Spencer slightly and he stammered for a reply. 'What do you do then?'

'What the fuck's it got to do with you? Listen pal, I've been courteous up to now, but you're beginning to bother me. Paisley's a small town, you'll see people more than once. Deal with it. Now if you don't mind.' Steele shooed him with his hand and eyebrows to walk on.

Spencer stumbled a couple of steps to the side, not being used to being spoken to in such a manner. He knew the two were police, and were following him. Why? If they had anything on him surely they would just arrest him? The boy? They'd take the word of a half cast bastard before his? Never? It wouldn't stand up. He walked on, past the bakers and the cash for gold shop, cursing the embarrassment of junkies that littered the street. If he had his way he'd round up the lot of them and air-drop them on Cumbrae or some other island, let them tear each other to bits instead of disturbing the lives of decent working folk. He looked over his shoulder, the two policemen were still stood at the tobacconist's window. He turned into the High Street and almost knocked over a Big Issue vendor. He swore savagely at him and continued up the street, scowling at the pathetic display of overhead Christmas lights, left up from last year. He would get that bastard, what was his name again? Harry had told him. He couldn't remember, it was immaterial, he was immaterial, expendable. He would soon find out that it didn't pay to mess with him. Small fry, he was sick of having to deal with the detritus of life day in day out, and now there was more to clean up. There was no way that joker was going to get anywhere near him again. What right did he have? Who the hell did he think he was? To talk to him like that? He wasn't looking where he was going and had just past yet another Charity Shop when he bumped into someone. 'Watch where...' he started but didn't finish as he saw that the person he had bumped into was a uniformed policeman.

'You should look where you're going sir,' the policeman said to him. 'You could get yourself into all sorts of bother not paying attention in this town.'

'Thanks for that,' Spencer replied curtly. 'I will.' He walked on, cursing quietly to himself.

'No need to apologise sir,' the officer shouted after him. 'All part of the service.'

There was no acknowledgement from Spencer that he had heard what was being said. The officer got on the radio to Steele and told him he was in pursuit.

Steele turned to Mansell, the two of them now idling their way back to the station. 'They'll watch him tonight and I think tomorrow we step it up a bit, make the prick sweat.'

'Sure,' Mansell agreed. 'He's an arrogant sod, isn't he?'

'Middle management council officials,' Steele snorted up some phlegm, thinking twice before expelling it unceremoniously down a drain in the roadside. 'Give them a bit of power and they think they're actually running the town. Jumped up bus inspectors. Don't suppose you fancy a pint?' he asked more in hope than anything else.

'For once you're wrong Robert,' Mansell slapped him on the back. 'Get your coat love, you've pulled.'

'Let's head back to The Last Post then,' Steele turned on his heels, leaving Mansell scratching his head.

'I thought you said that they...'

'I know what I said,' Steele grabbed at his shoulder. 'But they've a real ale special on this week.'

'What joy!' Mansell remarked. 'Real ale. There's a fair chance you'll be farting like a trooper come the morning then? In my car? Farting like a...'

'C'mon you, stop your whingeing.'

They hit The Last Post. They hit The Bull. They hit Bertie's. They hit Corkers and then The Tea Gardens before eventually hitting the kebab shop and a couple of taxis home.

50

Steele almost fell onto the linoleum as he opened the kitchen door. He was birling, the kebab falling from the wrapper as he forced it out in front to find the work surface. He planted the now cold kebab on the surface and opened the unit door and pulled out a glass and a bottle of whisky. It was a move he had rehearsed many times. He stuck the glass in his mouth and bit down on it as he carried the bottle and his soggily wrapped dinner through to the living room. He placed the glass, bottle and kebab on the side table and staggered towards the wall unit to hunt down a record. He squinted dramatically, trying to read the album title with his head tilted to the side. He knew it was red, maybe with a touch of black and grey. Bingo! He worked it loose with his link sausage fingers and placed Bruce Springsteen's Nebraska on the turntable. As the stylus scratched towards the title track Steele smirked and mumbled. 'Low fi! The big man was doing it years before any of these idiots were even born! Ha!' he slumped into his chair and poured himself a whisky, downing it in one.

'Often talk to yourself do you?' a voice behind him asked.

Steele turned, 'What the fuck?' he slurred. All of a sudden Ross Spencer was standing over him, his right hand clutching a bicycle lock and his left a seven-inch Sabatier knife. Ross Spencer led with the right and Steele saw stars.

51

It was Mansell's wife who heard the phone first, his phone, work phone. Why she was stumbling from her warm bed to find it in his jumble of clothes on the chair was a mystery to her. He had come in much the worse for wear, much more than he ever had before. Drunk and apologetic, saying sorry for everything – for being drunk, being late, having spent money he felt they could ill afford, for missing the girls' bath-time and bedtime stories, for spilling his kebab (a kebab! Of all things) on the kitchen floor. He didn't do it often, and had never to this extent. When he did get drunk, it was always with Rob Steele. Tonight, she got it out of him that it had been Rob Steele's fault again. (He had apologised for going out with him.) She didn't mind it as such, but it was the extent to which he was drunk that worried her – he couldn't remember some of the places he had been, what he had spoken about, how he had got home, whether there was any dinner or not? *"Have I had my dinner?"* he had repeatedly asked, instantly forgetting the incident with the flying kebab. He had eaten it after scooping it up off the floor, much to her chagrin. She could see the front light of the ringing phone illuminated through the pocket of his suit trousers and grabbed at them. The ringing was incessant, people normally hung up after a few rings, but this had been going on for about a minute now. She fished in the pocket and pulled out the phone. She pressed the green button and held it to her ear.

'He's gone Sir!' The voice on the other end sounded nervous and panicky. 'We think he's sneaked out through the back garden, but he's definitely not there.'

'I take it you want to speak to Detective sergeant Mansell?' Alice Mansell asked calmly. 'I'll see if I can rouse him for you, although it's highly unlikely, he's been out carousing with a certain Detective Inspector.' The tone of her voice sounded harsher than she had actually meant it to, she didn't resent him "cutting loose" as he so quaintly put it, it was just the short-term memory loss than disturbed her. She nudged her husband's left shoulder with the phone and stuck her finger in his left ear. He was instantly awake.

'What is it?' he mumbled. 'What's happened?'

She held the phone in front of his confused face. 'Phone.' She said coldly. 'For you!' She threw the phone on the bed and walked back round to her side.

He found the phone. 'Yes, speak,' Jesus, he thought, he sounded just like Steele did when he picked up a phone.

'We've lost him sir,' the voice repeated. 'We think he got out via the back garden, over the wall and into the neighbours.'

Mansell didn't know if he was on foot or horseback. 'Who is this? What are you talking about?' he asked through the foggy confusion.

'It's constable Fraser sir,' the voice croaked. 'Myself and WPC Mavers have been staking out the Spencer place in Elderslie and we couldn't see any sign of life, so we investigated further.'

Mansell was getting it now, the fog clearing. 'What do you mean you've "lost him"? How could you lose him?'

'Sorry sir, but we've investigated further and there's no sign of him in the house.'

'You've been in the house?'

'Yes sir,' he gulped.

'Did you talk to the wife?' Mansell asked.

'She away sir,' Fraser told him. 'The two boys also, at her mother's according to the neighbours.'

'So, were you in the house? Or just looking through the window?' Mansell didn't want to hear what he knew he was going to hear next.

'In the house sir,' Fraser gulped. 'We suspected he had absconded so we...'

'Entered the premises of a prime suspect without a warrant.' Mansell sighed and pulled back the duvet. Alice scowled beside him and pulled it closer into her. 'Bloody marvellous! Have you called DI Steele?'

'Tried sir,' Fraser answered. 'But he wasn't picking up. It just rang out.'

'Right,' Mansell got to his feet and realised he was naked. He normally wore pyjamas bottoms in bed in case one of the girls came in during the night. He must just have fell in. 'I'll phone DI Steele, and you two wait there in case he comes back. What a disaster.' He finished the call and searched his notebook for Steele's number. He called it and a disjointed voice told him that the phone he was trying to get through to had been switched off. He instantly knew something was amiss, Steele would never turn off the work phone at this stage of an investigation, no matter how drunk he was. And anyway, Fraser had said it was ringing out before. Someone other than Steele must have the phone. He switched on the light to get dressed. His wife threw a hardback tome at him and pulled the duvet over her head.

52

When Steele came to, he found he had been tied to one of the kitchen chairs with thick black cable ties – hands and feet. What was it with the police? He mused. It was only within the last few years that they had started replacing the cumbersome metal handcuffs with cable ties. Always one step behind. He looked around blearily. He was in his own living room, tidy for this time of night – the only record sleeve on the floor being Nebraska – the bleak landscape of the cover blurry to him. Then again, he had been unconscious, the single bare light bulb highlighting the blank loneliness of his life. At least the bulb was long-life. How long had he been unconscious? The record was still on, the sound having been obviously turned down by Spencer – he didn't look like the sort of guy who would appreciate The Boss – looked more of a Queen man, Steele almost laughed. He wondered if the album had gone on to repeat, as it did sometimes (he couldn't even control his stereo – what chance would he have with a computerised record collection?) How long had he been drifting solo through this life when he could have been happily shacked up with some comely wife to come home to in an evening, instead of this drinking nonsense? He made a note to slap himself when he next had use of his hands. He was still pissed and mentally babbling, needed to focus. Really focus, for he felt he would soon be fighting for his life. Again! This was getting to be a habit. He shook his head and looked behind, towards the door to the hallway. It was dark. Where was he? What did he have in mind? Was this waiting part of his torture process? Had he made Bob McLean and Georgina McBride wait like this while he decided in what sick and twisted way he was going to despatch them. He felt a wave of drunken guilt pour over him, he had completely forgotten about Angela James. He internally cursed himself and his working class background. The working/under class, those that lived on the fringes of society had become nothing to the police, the press and society in general. The only time they became prominent was when they killed – generally one of their own – and for a second a nation spluttered into its collective cornflakes. But only for a second. She had a life as well. Wasn't hers' a worthy existence in the same way in which Georgina McBride's had been? More worthy really, for she hadn't spent all her time screwing rich men into the ground at the behest of their bitter wives. She had just been unlucky, unlucky to have been born into her seemingly never ending spiral of poverty, benefits and unwanted pregnancies. He knew who he blamed for the underclass, but he was babbling again, fucking Grantham grocer's daughter. Again, he promised himself a slap. He stopped thinking and listened – what any good copper should do – look and listen. He could hear Spencer walking about upstairs, in his bedroom. What was he looking for in there? That room was as barren as the rest of his life. Another slap. How could he sober himself up and focus on the matter at hand if he had no access to water or coffee. Or more alcohol. He heard the footsteps move to the top of the stairs.

'Leettle pig! Leettle pig!' Spencer's voice sounded different from before. Detached, possessed. 'Are you there leettle pig? Papa wolf has something for you.'

Steele heard footsteps start to descend the stairs and felt two droplets of warm sweat run from his hairline to his neck.
'How you doing, Piggy?' Steele looked up and saw Ross Spencer leering at him from the doorway wearing only jeans, his gym-bought torso shaved and shining.
'You'll not get away with this you know,' Steele clutched at the only straw he had, his tongue. It had got him into trouble plenty in the past, but now he was relying on it to do the opposite.
'Why would that matter to you?' Spencer said coldly. 'You'll be dead.'
'That would be a mistake,' Steele tried to catch him with a look, but his eyes were idly wandering around the living room.
'For you, yes,' he laughed. 'For me? I'm not so sure.'

'Why?' asked Steele, the perspiration running from his hairline onto his thick eyebrows. 'Why Georgina McBride? Why Bob McLean? Why...'?

'Shut up pig!' Spencer lunged at him, the point of the knife poking at his Adam's apple. 'If you haven't worked it out, why should I tell you? Most people's idea of hell is to die wondering, well you just might be "most people". Tragic, eh?'

'Humour me just a little bit,' Steele pleaded, screwing up his nose at the halitosis coming from Spencer's mouth. His breath smelt of dog shit.

'Humour you?' he laughed, moving the knife round to his ear, the sharp point against his lobe like it was about to partake in some primitive piercing. 'I'll cut you. Slice your ear so that you can never listen to another snitch in your life. That's not what you call them though, is it? Is it "grass"? "Snout"? Anyway, whatever you call them, were you alive, you wouldn't be able to hear them.'

Steele was now more confused than terrified. 'I don't get it,' he frowned.

Spencer smiled broadly. 'You don't, do you? Too stupid. You're all too stupid. I mean, you were an afterthought, I wasn't going to touch you, didn't know of your existence, but you forced yourself upon me, you brought this on yourself.'

'But the others,' said Steele. 'What had they done to you?'

Spencer now laughed manically, his head and body shaking. 'They made me look a fool, an idiot with no control. That's what they did.'

'How?' asked a confused Steele.

'How?' Spencer spluttered incredulously. 'Every day I would read stories about how my brother was making a fool of himself. It was embarrassing. Totally embarrassing.'

'Vanity,' Steele snarled. 'You've caused all this, all this death and upset for all these people because they made you look bad by proxy? You fucking idiot!'

'Idiot? Me?' Spencer laughed. 'Am I tied to a chair awaiting my execution? I think not.'

'But why the cutting?' asked Steele. 'The tongue? The fingers? The vagina?'

'You really don't know? Don't know why I'm cutting off your ear?' Spencer jabbed the point of the blade into Steele's skin and he flinched dramatically. 'Because that's how you earn your living, listening to grasses and victims and acting on their pathetic snivelling words. She was the same, McBride, only with her it was her tongue that peddled the lies – in courts, in letters. And McLean, every time his fingers touched a keyboard the lies just flowed.' Spencer looked round towards the window, he was sure he'd seen a car draw up.

'They weren't lies,' Steele began, feeling the tip of the blade cut at the back of his ear. 'Your brother needed help and all you could think of to do for him was to murder people he'd come into contact with. You killed the bloody woman he loved,' he reminded him. 'How is that doing anybody any good? Argh!' Steele squealed as he felt the knife cut though his skin.

'She was embarrassing him,' he scowled, the knife inching towards the hanging lobe. He looked around at the window and saw the neon of silently flashing blue police lights reflected on the windows of the house opposite. 'McBride was embarrassing him, slut,' he spat. 'And that fat bastard McLean had made a laughing stock of him. I did it for him, but did the...'

'Embarrassing you, more like? Jesus!' The pain was intense, but he had to talk his way out of this. 'Who the hell do you think you are? Vain basta...' The last thing he heard was final line from the song "Highway Patrolman" – *"A man turns his back on his family, well he just ain't no good."* A faint smile crossed his face as he faded into unconsciousness.

53

Mansell had no choice other than to call it in. Get every available uniform – which was a dozen (cuts, cuts, everywhere) – and get them to round to Steele's home address as soon as... sooner if they could. No point in beating about the bush, he was one of their own, no time to waste, even if it was a fool's errand and they got there only to find D.I. Steele with his head and his hands down his puke-filled toilet trying to fish out a mobile phone. Mansell had always been a belt and braces man, and this was no time to get gallus. If he was in trouble he would thank him, if not he'd chew his ear off. As he got into his car he knew it was a chance he would take, and he would happily accept the bollocking. Just so long as the curmudgeonly old sod was still in one piece. He had faith in him – when he was sober, but the state he was in, the state they were in, he noted, jumping the lights on the junction of Neilston Road and Canal Street. He roared past the maisonettes to his right and the fire station to his left. The lights were also red at the junction where George Street crossed with Maxwellton. He slowed the car to a crawl as he approached, knowing the West End of the town to be filled with loons, pedestrian and in vehicles. He rounded the kidney-shaped Ferguslie Roundabout on the wrong side and was at the next roundabout in less than ten seconds. He hadn't had time to think about how drunk he still was; all he knew was that he was needed. Needed by his boss, by his friend. The thought sobered him slightly and he took the roundabout at a snail's pace.

As he turned into Phoenix Drive the air was blue with silent sirens. He noted the ambulance parked to the side of Steele's house and abandoned his car without switching off the engine and ran inside expecting the worst. He almost fell on the gravel pathway that lead to the front door and actually *did* fall over the step and into the hallway. 'Boss!' he hollered as he stopped his chin hitting the carpet by millimetres. From his prone position all he could see was a clump of pressed black trousers and Doctor Martins. He looked upwards and saw four pairs of eyes staring back down at him, the laughter barely suppressed.

'Is that my young sparring partner come to see how his auld mucker is?' Steele bellowed from the living room.

Mansell got to his feet with all the dignity of a drunken camel and entered the living room. A paramedic was bandaging the back of Steele's left ear. 'Sir,' he spluttered, glad he wasn't too late.

Steele caught his nervousness and tried to put him at his ease. 'Better late than never, you could be looking at "the deceased" if these lads,' he nodded to the uniforms, 'hadn't been so diligent. Don't know who called them in, but I'd like to buy him a drink.'

'Maybe wait until we capture Spencer first sir?' Mansell walked towards his boss, resisting the urge to grab at him, to cuddle him, to feel his life force. 'What's the news on that? What exactly happened sir?' Mansell nodded at the ear the paramedic was binding with glue. Steele told him exactly what had happened since they had separated at the taxi rank in Gilmour Street. 'So, he's either on foot or riding a bike?' Mansell surmised. 'Shouldn't be too hard to spot. We'll call in the eye in the sky.'

Steele went to shake his head, but flinched as the paramedic held his head fixed. 'Pilot's off sick,' he informed Mansell. 'I got one of these lads to try control and that's what they told him. Marvellous, eh?'

'Surely there's a standby pilot?' proffered Mansell.

'Now's not the time to ponder on the vagaries of the police helicopter budget,' Steele began, laughing to himself. 'But to get on foot, on horseback, car if all else fails, and catch the bastard. Fuck all this slowly slowly catchy monkey business. We've got him, he'll squeal just for the publicity. An ego that could fill Hampden.'

'I think maybe you should come with me to the hospital sir,' the paramedic started. 'You've had a nas...'

'Stitch me up and leave me be.' Snapped Steele. 'You've got your work to do and so have I.'

'I can only tell you what...'

'Sorry,' Steele apologised. 'Sorry mate, but I'm not going to that hospital again. Thanks for all your help though. Are we done.'

The paramedic straightened up to his six foot four inches and took off his blue gloves 'No problem, hope you catch him.'

'When you're ready sir,' Mansell eyed the window. 'The car's still running.'

'What! You left the engine...'

Mansell ran outside to the spot where he'd abandoned his car, grateful it was still there, billowing exhaust fumes into the night air.

54

Steele stood in front of DCI Bain, his blotchy face about to burst with the anger he was suppressing. The night search had proved long and fruitless, and Steele and Mansell stood before their superior tired, unshaven and reeking of the previous nights' drink. Spencer was still at large. Steele stole a glance at the council building opposite – just over fifty yards away. They could have leant over and collared him while he sat at his desk. Right under their bloody copper's noses. A ridiculous state of affairs that they had made a total arse of, to put it bluntly. Repeatedly arresting the wrong brother – they only had bloody two to choose from! It wasn't that that riled Bain so much.

'One bloody pilot and if he calls in a sicky we're screwed.' He ran his hand over his bald head, his hat tightly and angrily gripped by the fingers of his left hand. 'It's positively Dickensian, this is modern policing for God's sake.'

The two men let him rant without interruption, unsure as to whether the extra strong mints they were both sucking on were having any effect on the fruity fumes emitting from their mouths. When they did speak, they positioned their faces and the direction of their breath downwards. Steele was a past master at this type of conversation, but Mansell was catching on quickly. Bain read their body language wrongly, thought they were ashamed that they had Spencer, but had allowed him to evade their grasp.

He patted Steele's bicep. 'No need for you to feel bad about this Rob,' he coughed, uncomfortable with the physical contact. 'He's a slippery bugger all right. Not to mention dangerous. You lads go and get some kip, uniform are buzzing like wildfire out there. If he surfaces, we'll have him.'

'Maybe an hour or so sir,' Steele conceded. 'But then I think we'd rather get back in the field. He's nearly sliced my ear off. I don't want him getting to anyone else.'

'Fair enough Rob,' Bain replaced his hat on his head. 'If it wasn't for these damned meetings I'd be out there myself. No doubt the chopper pilot from Inverclyde will arrive shortly, that will help us out.'

'Thank you sir,' Steele stepped back and headed for his office. Mansell followed. 'Get our heads down on the desk for an hour or so, what do you reckon,' he said over his shoulder.

'I had better phone Alice first,' Mansell gulped. 'Otherwise I'm liable to go home next and find the locks changed.'

Steele cackled like Popeye. 'Ach, tell her you're a polis and that if she doesn't like it she can straighten her face and lump it. Kidding son, kidding.'

Mansell knew he was and laughed. 'Aye, I'll just put her straight boss. Maybe give her a wee backhander.'

'Women,' Steele held the door to the office open for him. 'I don't envy you.'

They two men sat on their chairs and slumped into their desks exhaustedly.

An hour or so later they were awoken abruptly by the entrance of Sarinder Kapoor into the office. 'My God, Robert Steele,' He wafted his hand in front of his face and went over to open a window. 'Smells like a blooming brewery in here old man.' He turned his attention to Mansell. 'And I see you are leading this young man astray. Tut tut. Did your mother never warn you of such depravity?' He walked across and opened another window, looking over at the council building. 'I hear our killer was under our very noses all this time.'

'He was that,' Steele got to his feet and smoothed down his trousers. 'We could have reached out and touched him, grabbed him by the throat and pulled him into a cell.'

'And you have no idea where he is now?' Kapoor added.

'CCTV are onto it,' Steele informed him. 'Though, that's proved to be a total washout so far.' He thought back to his assault in Central Way and the sprayed over camera on the road down from the Braes. 'We're not holding our breath. Pounding the beat seems to be the most reliable option.'

'Good to hear it.' Kapoor chided. 'For I think you are still too far over the limit for driving.'

'He's driving,' Steele pointed at Mansell.

'Thought we were *pounding the*...' Mansell was stopped in his tracks.

'Figure of speech. Why bark when you've a dog to do it for you.' Steele smirked.

'Dog?' Mansell asked. 'When did I get promoted?'

'Anyway Sarinder, was this a social call or is there something we can do for you?' asked Steele.

'Oh no, purely social. I was passing and...' he drifted off, his eyes staring across at the council building. Steele tracked his line of vision. 'That is him? Is it not? Ross Spencer?'

Steele couldn't believe what he was seeing, the gall of the man. 'Bastard!' he muttered incredulously. 'What an absolute bastard.' Spencer was in his office, rooting through his desk for something. He spotted Steele staring at him and carried on looking in his desk. He appeared to find it and walked over to the window. He waved at Steele and made a slicing motion to his ear with a knife before exiting his office.

'How the hell did he get in there? Have we not got someone staking that place out? Amateurs. Come on son, looks like we're on foot after all.

55

Amateurs, he thought, a total waste of breath. All he needed was a schemie skip hat and the flatfoots didn't look at him twice as he breezed past them and into the customer services foyer before walking through the back door to the stairs. There was no way he was taking the lift, it had broken down too many times, and anyway, he had to keep moving, the adrenaline whizzing through his blood making him feel that if he stopped he would self-combust. He took the stairs two at a time and didn't see a soul in the corridor as he made his way to the office. It was all falling apart and he had to make good his exit. He knew he had lost everything, there was no chance of a reconciliation now. He almost smirked. He'd have to disappear out of their lives. It was too soon though, he needed more time, at least one more kill. He swiped and entered his office. You'd have thought the Mill Street Monkeys would at least have put someone up here, not just the wet behind the ears idiot outside the buildings. Talking of which…He saw straight into Steele's office, him and the guy in the blue suit were talking to someone he hadn't seen before. Positive discrimination, they were everywhere. There'd be another vacancy as soon as he saw off that smug bastard Steele. Why hadn't he simply plunged him last night and be done with it? It hadn't felt right, he had needed more time to do the job right. He was never one for cutting corners. Steele's time would come, he'd finish him off before he bade farewell to this shitty stinking town. London Calling. Plenty of opportunities for a man with his talents in the big smoke. Easy to disappear and become just another face, anonymous with all the other nameless millions. Look at that idiot Steele trying to stare him down. He found the keys to the lock up and his seldom used motorbike in his desk – a rudimentary schoolboy error, but he was allowed one. He should have kept everything close at hand should the need ever arise to take flight. He hadn't expected it to be so soon though. He stood up and pulled the knife from his pocket. Last night was just a warning the real show's just about to start. Flight, definitely flight. He bolted down the corridor and took the stairs three at a time on the way down, and walked purposefully through the customer services and out the disabled exit. He felt like giving the flatfoot a wave as he headed for the Abbey, but he needed to buy himself more time. When he felt he was far enough away he broke into a trot.

56

Steele and Mansell got round to the front of the council buildings before any squad cars turned up. Steele grabbed at the lapels of the uniformed officer. 'You've let him in, tell me you haven't let him out as well?' The young officer looked confused and was saved by Mansell tapping Steele on the shoulder.

'Is that him sir?' He pointed and Steele turned just in time to see Spencer disappear down the pedestrian walkway between the Abbey and the Town Hall. The two men set off in pursuit leaving the uniformed officer wondering what he should do now.

'Is that prick not following us?' gasped Steele.

Mansell turned and waved the officer to follow them. 'He is now sir.'

'Jesus!' Steele panted. 'Remind me to go teetotal.' His feet felt heavy on the mono-blocking as they got to the Abbey and looked about for Spencer. He could have disappeared into the Abbey or the town hall, thinking they wouldn't look there, or more likely towards the shopping precinct. If they had known what he was looking for in his office they might have some clue as to where he was heading, but he was currently running into the busy town centre with a six-inch knife in his hand, intent on a killing spree for all they knew. They stopped between the gap in the two buildings.

'What do you think sir?' Mansell eyed the two buildings.

'Nah, too enclosed.' He replied. 'He's going somewhere.'

The uniformed officer caught up with them. 'Sorry sir,' he gasped.

Steele pointed towards The Piazza. 'He went that way,' the officer set off immediately and Steele had to shout after him. 'He's armed!' The two men followed the younger policeman.

'He's tanking at some speed,' Mansell commented.

'Fit and thick, just what the modern police force needs,' scowled Steele as they stopped at the traffic lights opposite The Piazza. Steele phoned in for all available back up to get off their backsides and onto the streets. He wanted the place buzzing with uniformed officers. He wanted this finished before there was any more bloodshed.

'What do you think sir?' asked Mansell.

'We split up son,' he replied. 'You run round the other side of The Piazza and I'll head up the High Street. Keep your phone live.' Steele headed off towards the war memorial, its steps teeming with the usual collection of junkies, drunks and hopeless cases. He had no time to scowl at them, nor at the fact that the Christmas lights from last year were still up, the council workers too busy in the bookies to take them down. His eyes were everywhere, scanning the street up as far as Orr Square. Spencer was nowhere to be seen. If he had gone this way he had gone inside one of the shops, probably The Paisley Centre, more exits and nooks and crannies to hide in. He brushed past the leaflet distributors and into the centre. He scanned the burger bar, chocolate shop, Chinese healer, Phone shop, all the while his steps measured, not actually running and not actually walking, trotting almost. He checked the charity shop, pound shop, and the couple of chemists. There was every chance he had gone back on himself and snuck through Marks and Spencers and back onto the High Street – if he was in here at all. He stared ahead about fifty feet to the escalators and saw the top of a black Nike hat begin its descent on the stairs. He took a chance on it being Spencer and broke into a sprint, knocking aside an overweight monkey in a cheap suit trying to harangue him into changing his gas and electric supplier. He had no time to apologise, simply pulled out his warrant card and held it up above his head as he rounded the stairwell. He looked down and saw Spencer's blond hair poking out the back of the hat. He spoke into the phone. 'Dave, Dave, you there?' he heard a muffled reply, Mansell's voice breathless from running. 'He's in the Paisley Centre. First floor, the one with all the wee stalls. You hear me? Go softly, softly. I don't want a bloodbath.'

'Right boss,' answered Mansell. 'I'll call it in, get all the exits covered.'

Steele stuck his warrant card in his inside jacket pocket and made his way down the escalator, eyes all the while on his target. He had stopped at the first of the In-shops that sold second hand telephones and sim cards. He must have felt Steele's gaze burning a hole in his hat, for he turned and looked directly at him. He looked to his left as well and Steele followed his line of vision. A uniformed WPC was talking into her shoulder as she approached Spencer. He immediately turned on his heels and ran. So much for softly, softly, Steele scowled, pushing people aside as he headed for the bottom of the stairs. He caught the WPC before she started running after Spencer. It was Mhairi McKay. 'No heroics! He's armed,' he barked breathlessly. 'Don't approach him until back up gets here.'

'Sir,' she replied, a look of fear suddenly in her eyes.

'That way,' Steele pointed in the direction that Spencer had headed in. 'I'll cut through,' he pointed to the middle of the three entrances to the In Shops. 'Try and block him in.' The In shops were a labyrinth of room-sized shops that sold things that wouldn't support a business on the High Street. Wool, big knickers, bargain basement meat, a pet shop, a fortune teller. The Barra's in miniature. As Steele passed a shoe shop and one that sold nothing but puzzle books he saw the blur of blond run by towards the fortune teller and one of the two cafes.

At the junction of the café and pet shop he paused and looked to his right, his eyes giving away the fact that he didn't frequent this mini maze very often. He was looking for an exit and turned into the café. A dead end, thought Steele, upping his step. He made the entrance to the café in time to see Spencer stare at a chained fire door. Cornered, going nowhere.

Spencer turned and saw Steele, his expression a mix of frustration and evil. Saliva poured freely from his mouth as he spoke. 'Ah, little pig,' he pulled the knife from his pocket. 'Unfinished business I think.' He began running towards Steele who grabbed a table and held it up to defend himself.

Panic spread through the café, the diners screaming, shouting and gasping at proceedings. All except for one man who was busy tapping a slice of rock-hard black pudding on his plate and staring in an annoyed fashion towards the catering staff.

Spencer lunged at the table, the hat falling from his head, his lion's mane hair distracting Steele from the knife. Steele batted at him with the table and struck his shoulder. Mhairi McKay rounded the corner by the pet shop and straight into Spencer. She went to grab him, but he had regained his composure and stabbed her side, just under her ribs. She looked confused as she fell to the ground. Steele grabbed at the table again, held a metal leg and threw it at Spencer's head. Spencer batted it off with his knife hand and once more lunged at the policeman, his hand above his head as he forced the knife downwards. Steele made to turn and it ripped at his shoulder. The pain was instant.

'ARMED POLICE!' A voice roared. 'DROP YOUR WEAPON!'

Spencer was stood over the prone Steele and turned to look down the alleyway to where the shout had come from. As he did Steele pulled back his leg and booted him heavily between the legs. 'Basic schoolboy error,' he gasped getting to his feet as Spencer reeled backwards. Steele looked to where the shout had come and there was Mansell, a policeman alright, but seriously unarmed. He began running towards the mêlée. Spencer staggered into a display hamster cage outside the pet shop and started towards the oncoming Mansell, the knife brandished firmly in his hand.

'Come on pig!' he hollered. 'Come on!' With the handle of the knife he battered heavily on one of the two large tanks, one filled with tropical fish the other with goldfish. It shattered instantly, a cascade of water and tropical fish filling the floor. He did the same with the second tank to the same effect. As Mansell approached he slipped on half a dozen fish and his backside hit the floor before he knew what was happening. Spencer was running towards him, the knife slashing like a windmill in a hurricane. It sliced across his arm as he held it up to defend himself. He awaited a second lunge but it never arrived. He turned from his prone position and saw Spencer running towards the stairwell. He looked back and saw Steele tending to a WPC. It didn't look good.

Steele caught his blank look and shook his head slowly. 'Get him Dave.' He gasped softly. 'Get him.'

Mansell steadied himself and got uneasily to his feet. He ran towards the escalators, the public cowering. He saw the egresses filling with uniforms and some fifteen feet ahead of him Spencer looking frantically this way and that. Dave Mansell knew he was looking for a hostage, some innocent to shield him from the weight of police. Dave Mansell was not going to let that happen. He looked to the wall and pulled the fire extinguisher from its cradle with his good arm. He launched it through the air and it caught Spencer in the small of his back. He was felled instantly, the knife dropping from his hand. He felt the weight of the police within seconds.

57

The next day in Mill Street there was a strangely subdued atmosphere, the death of a colleague, especially a well-liked WPC like Mhairi, larger than any euphoria felt at a collar in the biggest case ever to pollute the station. No champagne corks popped, no chink chink of whisky glasses or puffing of cigars all round. Barely a word was spoken that wasn't necessary.

'A difficult day Robert, David.' DCI Bain stood over Steele and Mansell as they sat at their desk, their wounded arms in slings. 'Very difficult.'

'Yes sir,' they said in unison.

'She was a single child, elderly parents. I think this will finish them off.' He exhaled and tapped at his pursed lips with his index fingers. 'Tragic. But let's not take anything away from what you guys did. Commendable. Good work.' Bain almost smiled, but held it back and made for the door. He paused and turned. 'Oh, and there's some good news about the shoe pervert. Apparently, there's some crazed driving instructor in Dykebar babbling ten to the dozen, confessing everything. I'm sending those useless beggars McGlaughlin and Patterson up. A mixed day I would say.' He exited the office without waiting for a reply.

'A mixed day?' Steele sighed at Mansell.

'Let's get a drink.' Suggested Mansell. 'I'll just call my wife first.'

Steele struggled to get his jacket over his bandaged arm and again sighed. 'A mixed day, by Christ!'

Continue to read a sneak preview of the next book in Tony McLean's **Paisley Patterns** series;

"From Guy Fawkes to Remembrance"

From Guy Fawkes to Remembrance

Imagine

Paisley was a town on its knees begging to be shot and put out of its misery. It was a three-legged dog hobbling down the mercantile avenue on the lookout for sadistic snipers in the trees. Snipers who would happily dispatch a bullet into its remaining back leg and watch as it hilariously attempted to keep going by crawling and scraping its bony backside along the pavement. With the passing of each week the owners of the once affluent mill town's shops bit on their own bullets and shut their doors, seemingly forever. Within another couple of weeks their shop fronts would have been given the "imagine" treatment by the council's marketing department. Full size glossy photographs would be erected to cover the whole of their frontage, leaving no gaps so that the misery and pain that had once lurked within could be neither seen nor felt. No, the "imagined" shops were supposed to give hope and encourage more investment in the town, just different ventures from what had been there before.

"Imagine your toy shop here!" A two hundred-seater burger bar was now an imagined toy shop, old fashioned Jack in the Boxes and dolls staring ghoulishly out at the passing shoppers. It had been an "imagined" toy shop longer than it had ever been a burger bar.

"Imagine your bakery here!" A shoe shop was now an "imagined" artisan bakery with loaves and buns from every country in Europe glazed and glistening on The High Street. Not a pie in sight! Any artisan baker foolhardy enough to take on the

established pie and bridie vendors in the town deserved to lose their dough.

It was getting to the stage that when a shop closed its doors the good burghers of Paisley began to wonder what the art department would imagine it to be. They had recently embraced the shifting immigration and had "imagined" both a Polish delicatessen and Butchers. Amazingly, both shops had opened up and were currently going concerns. Was this the upturn in fortune the town was looking for? Only time would tell. The only other shops opened within the last three years were Barbers, nail bars and those selling legal highs.

So, the town centre was on its knees but trying to rise again. To the south of the centre a different type of problem had arisen. Rumour had it there was a beast loose on the Glennifer Braes, scaring the dog walkers and terrorising the Highland cattle.

Here we go folks, strap in!

Saturday

1.

For the best part of a week the stench from the Cart tannery was the worst it had been for years. Its' unpleasant tang enveloping most of the town centre and as far south as Saint Sausalito's Roman Catholic church. Today was Bonfire Night and the gunpowder and cordite of the fireworks had banished the smell of the rotting carcasses, at least for a little while. Inside, the chapel the smells were the usual, incense and candles, but the main aroma was that of untreated damp – Fifty-three years of rain would do that to the sturdiest of structures. Even those protected by God. It wasn't just damp, it was freezing too, the heating system never having been updated since the original chapel had been erected.

Father Finbar Finnegan was sat in his confessional awaiting the next confessor. So far it had been all the "doubting my faith" and "impure thoughts" that were unfortunately never expanded upon. He had a tartan blanket covering his legs and wore two black sweaters to keep the cold from his chest. He stamped his feet on the concrete floor as the next parishioner came through the door. He peered through the grate. Here we go again! He thought. On the other side of the modesty grill Lucinda Lewington struggled to get down to the kneeler. She was a product of her times, Hammer Horror make-up coupled with a Monster Munch diet. She was twenty-four years of age and four foot seven in height, weighing in at eighteen stone three pounds in her stocking soles. This week she favoured vivid pink hair, make-up, as usual, trowelled, not just on to her face, but to the exposed parts of her breasts – of which there was a bounteous amount. Despite her still tender age she had once been a star, but was now nothing more than a distant memory to the public at large. 'Hello Father,' she huffed as her knees finally settled in position. Her face was almost touching the grill, the anonymous sanctity of the confessional lost forever as she shook her pink hair backwards then forwards. Father Finbar felt the barrier between them rock.

'How can I help you my dear?'

'Bless me father, for I have sinned,' Lucy puffed. 'It's been seven days since my last confession.' She paused and sighed heavily. 'It's me Father – Lucy Lewington.'

'I know Lucy, I know.' Finbar said. 'You've come to confess your sins?' It was never that easy. Lucy used the confessional, and him, as a form of therapy. The Hollywood stars all had their thousand dollars an hour therapist, burnt out star Lucy Lewington had Saint Sausalito's Father Finbar Finnegan free of charge.

'Well, yes,' she sighed again, this time it was forced. 'I'm not sure that God's listening to me Father. You know me Father, I'm a good God-fearing, good-living catholic.' She waited a second for affirmation.

Father Finbar murmured as his eyes rolled into the back of his head. They then checked his watch. Fifteen minutes before the Vigil mass. 'Was there anyone else waiting for confession before you came in Lucy?'

'No Father,' she replied. 'Just me.'

'Good, carry on.'

'Well, is he listening? God, I mean?' her voice trembled. 'What I want isn't so much to ask for Father. I just want what everybody else has. Is that so bad Father?'

'Lucy,' there was a sigh lurking in Finbar's throat but he held it at bay. 'What you're asking for is not something that would come from God. God has given you the means – your wonderful singing voice - with which to seek out what you want. The record deals and the fame that comes with it are yours to search for. But I hope you're not just seeking fame for fame's sake. That's vanity Lucy, in God's eyes...'

'I'm not vain Father,' Lucy replied. 'I mean, you've just got to look at me to see that.'

Finbar looked through the grate at the candyfloss atop Lucy's head and sighed audibly.

'I'm not Father, I just want what everyone else has.'

'But not everyone is famous, or wants to be famous Lucy.' Finbar had been espousing the same rhetoric to Lucy for the past year, but it didn't seem even to go in one ear in order to come out the other. 'You had your moment in the sun and now it's time to let someone else have a crack at it. These days fame is fleeting Lucy, blink and you miss it.'

'I mean, did you see that girl last week, the one that butchered the Celine Dion number?'

She was awaiting an answer. After a year she was still wanting an answer! 'No, as I've said on many occasions Lucy, I don't really watch much television.'

'Well she got through to the next round,' Lucy sounded astounded. 'To the boot camp!'

'Is this on *See The Stars*?' Father Finbar asked, he at least knew their names, if not their contents.

'No, honestly!' Lucy chided him. 'That's not on any more. This was Quest for Fame, you know with him that was big in the sixties and made a comeback thanks to...'

For the next ten minutes he let her prattle on about the unfairness of it all, about how her single – "A Thousand Stars", in the charts for four weeks - peaking at number two - had over a hundred thousand plays on a streaming website and how she hadn't gotten a penny from it, etcetera etcetera. He listened with half of one ear and moved his rosary between his fingers as he prayed silently. He too had things to confess – had done for years – but telling them would cost him his job, his calling. He looked through the grill as Lucy's mouth continued with its' tirade. As he started on his second batch of Hail Mary's he heard the tone of her speech patterns change, so he zoned in again.

'It's not so much that I have to confess what I've done,' she paused and Father Finbar cleared his throat to let her know he was still listening. 'It's what I'm about to do that I need to confess Father, it's what I'm about to do...'

Printed in Great Britain
by Amazon